WILDERNESS

Some shadows never let go.

Hunter Swanson

Cover design by Youness Elh
Edited by Angela Brown
First Edition
ISBN: 979-8-9999797-0-4

For the misunderstood youth:
You are not alone. Your pain is seen, and your story
matters.

In loving memory of my father,
a teacher who lit the way for so many.
You inspired greatness in your students—and in me.
Thank you for helping me become the man I am today.

Message from the Author

This is a horror novel for young adults. It explores mental health struggles, loss, and fear—both imagined and real. If you need to take breaks while reading, please do so. Take care of yourself first.

Chapter 1

It's been ten years, five months, and nineteen days since Mr. Shadow killed my dad, and here I am on a worn beige sofa staring at a glass-blown pumpkin placed between Dr. Samantha Hane's desktop and engraved nameplate. It's the only decorative piece in her entire office. She doesn't even have a motivational poster of a majestic lion or scenic mountain range with a clichéd quote at the bottom. What's so important about the pumpkin? Did she make it? Did a family member? A patient? I've tried asking the good psychiatrist about it, but the answer is always the same: "We are not here about me. This time is for you."

My attention wanders to the framed academic honors that adorn the wall behind Dr. Hane's desk, showcasing her prestigious résumé and highlighting why my mom selected her. I know to the right is a window overlooking Cedar Hills Forest, but I don't care much for the view. Unfortunately there's no clock to stare at since most teens use it as a challenge to stay quiet the whole session. To the left of my couch is a filled bookshelf with potted plants as bookends. I don't dare turn that way. Instead I stare at the wooden coffee table between Dr. Hane and me, debating if I should distract myself with one of the mandala coloring books stacked in the center.

"I know this is hard, Cody, but you're doing great."

I glance up and catch her kind hazel eyes urging me to continue. Dr. Hane brushes her shoulder-length auburn hair behind one ear and adjusts her cat-eye glasses. Out of all the psychiatrists I've had, she's the most stylish in her gray sleeveless overcoat and a white blouse tucked into wine-red pants cuffed above tan ankle-high boots. Although she's around my mom's age, she doesn't dress like it. Maybe she could give Mom some pointers for her job interview tomorrow.

Dr. Hane leans forward in her soft lavender accent chair with pen and pad in hand. "Let's continue. You arrived at the site. Your parents were setting up camp."

I take a deep breath, close my eyes, and dive back into the ten-year-old memory.

I was sitting in a green mesh folding chair with my sketchbook and colored pencils, trying to draw a shimmering translucent turtle-shelled squirrel preening its fluffy tail on a Douglas fir branch above my head. The small light spirit looked like a living iridescent bubble flowing with all the colors of the rainbow. I sketched the creature as fast as my little fingers could go, but the colored pencils Mom had packed weren't enough. The hardest part was getting the squirrel's shell just right because the pattern kept shifting.

Dr. Hane's voice brings me back to her office. "What were you doing?"

"Drawing a squirrel." It's best to leave out certain details, such as the shell and the fact the squirrel was a glittering light spirit. I don't even bother telling the good doctor about all the light spirits I saw that day. There was a flock of raccoons flying in formation on either side of the car on the way to the campsite. A small family of colorful deer with long peacock tails stood next to our parking spot when we arrived. A lizard with floppy ears was sunbathing on a rock behind the firepit before it scampered off as Mom almost dropped the wood on top of it. A slinky fox with three extra tails and budding antlers even came from the bushes and nuzzled against my leg before bounding back into the woods. Those are the kinda details I've learned to omit.

"Anything special about the squirrel?" Dr. Hane has her pen at the ready.

"Nope." I've seen enough shrinks to know when they're fishing. Plus she has my file. More like a novella at this point. Every psychologist, psychiatrist, counselor, nurse, doctor, judge, even my own mother doesn't want to hear the truth. They want "normal." There's no point in bringing up the spirits I see. No one believes me. At best I end up sitting on a beige sofa talking to another bespectacled professional who wants to get to know the *real me*. Instead I leave out any supernatural details and delve back into the memory.

Mom waddled over with her hands on her lower back to support her pregnant belly. When she passed under the branch, the turtle squirrel got spooked and disappeared up the tree.

"You scared it away," I grumbled.

Mom brushed her long, wavy dark hair to the side and glanced up before turning back with a fake sad face. She still pretended to see them. "I'm sorry. What are you working on?"

"It's not done." I tried to hide my drawing, but she took it anyway.

"Oh, it's beautiful. Are you sure you're only seven? Honestly you get the talent from your father. I have nowhere near the imagination you two do."

I just huffed and took my sketchbook back. There was no point trying to convince her that what I saw was real. She never believed me and never will. At least Dad did.

There was a hard crunch and a string of slurs. Dad threw the hammer down and sucked on his thumb, kicking the last spike to the tent.

Mom gave him a death glare. "Really, Dave?"

"Sorry." Dad shook the large tent. It stayed standing. Victorious, he brushed his hands off on his dirty jeans and joined us. "Your castle awaits, Queen Linda. A spacious one-bedroom with an open-concept living room, kitchen, and bathroom. Perfect for a soon-to-be family of five and this spare tire." He gave his stomach a little pat.

Mom smirked and shook her head. "I think your dad bod's cute."

He wrapped a supportive arm around Mom's waist and gave her a kiss.

"Seriously?" I pretended to gag a little.

"You should see Cody's newest creation," Mom said as Dad helped her to the tent. "What you two can come up with—"

"I'm not making it up!" Fed up with her, I threw the pencils into the dirt and stormed off.

Dr. Hane taps the end of her pen against the notepad, bringing me back to the couch. "What happened after your mom saw your drawing?"

"She took it to show my dad. I got pissed and left."

"What about the drawing or her showing it to your father made you so upset?"

Oh, Dr. Hane is good. Another line cast into the water, but I'm not biting. Been hooked too many times to fall for that again. I wish I could say I was upset because I wasn't a liar. Because I didn't make it up. Because what I see is real. But Mom never believed me, no matter how many times I tried. Just because she can't see light spirits doesn't mean they aren't real.

But if I have any hope of getting out of this constant cycle of assessments and medication, I need to give them what they want: a normal teenager. "I guess I felt she was making fun of me."

More quick notes. "Very good, Cody. Please continue."

"Dad chased after me to talk," I say as I lean back, close my eyes, and dive back into that godforsaken forest.

Dad chugged after me. "I got him. Little man and I need to have a man-to-man talk."

"Just stay close," Mom warned. "You don't know what's out there."

When he caught up to me, he wrapped me in his arms, attacking my ticklish spots. "Don't worry. If anything comes for us, I'll sacrifice Cody. It'll take at least five minutes to eat him up."

"Dad, stop!" I struggled. "I can't…breathe!" He relented and put me down. I paid him back with a playful punch to the thigh.

"Let's have a chat before it gets too dark." Together we headed into the woods.

We trekked until we reached a cliff that overlooked Olympic National Park. An ocean of trees stretched as far as I could see. The setting sun colored the sky a vibrant array of oranges and purples. A group of gliding otters played on the wind, glittering like crystals. A few took notice of us and drifted in our direction. Their chirps and squeaks were like clattering driftwood and seashell wind chimes.

"There's something you don't see in the city." Taking a seat in the grass, Dad patted the earth next to him. I joined and he pulled me close. "Listen, buddy, don't be so hard on your mom. She's not like you and me. We see the world a little differently than everyone else."

"Why don't you tell her you see and hear them too?"

Dad took a big breath before answering. "I used to, but…it made her worry, so I stopped. She has a hard time believing things she can't see."

"Why can't she?"

"Not sure. My guess is it's genetic. Like how you and I have the same bright-blue eyes. Maybe they help us see the things we do." Mom called our eyes "electric blue." No one else had such intense bright color like us. "But sometimes people have a hard time with things that are different from them. But being different isn't a bad thing. It makes you special. I know what it's like to feel alone with this. You know you can always talk to me."

The carefree otters played in the gentle breeze and drifted toward us. A few curious heads glanced in our direction, intrigued by the two visitors watching them dance in the sky. I got the distinct impression they were looking at me.

Dad rested a hand on my shoulder. "Did I ever tell you when your mother was pregnant with you, spirits started following her everywhere? She had no idea of course, but I could see them. Through the grocery store. When she left for work. Walks by the beach were my personal favorite. I didn't realize they were actually following you until you were born. It's as if spirits are drawn to you, Cody. It's incredible. You are very special. Never forget that."

The spirit otters bobbed and weaved through the air, their bodies moving with an elegant grace while their heads stayed locked on me. Only a few yards away, the family came to a sudden halt. Synchronized and on high alert, they darted their heads up to face the woods behind us like prey catching wind of a predator.

The hair on my arms stood on end, and the smell of sulfur washed over me, stinging my eyes and throat. I was suddenly submerged in the deep end of a frozen swimming pool.

With a jolt, the flock darted off in all different directions.

Dad put a protective arm around me. I felt it in his grip—he was spooked too. "Come on. Let's get back to Mom before—"

He stopped, gaze fixed forward. He was confused, but there was something else too. Something I'd never seen. Eyes wide and unblinking. Jaw clenched. Short staggered breaths. Dad was scared.

I strained to follow his gaze to the woods, but I couldn't make out anything through the long shadows. Another chill clicked down my spine. Nothing was there. All the animals, even the light spirits, were gone. The woods were dead silent.

That's when I saw him. A towering figure, darker than the shadows, slinked between the trees toward us. A person made of black mist. Another wave of burning odor washed over me. This shadow man was the source of the burning odor.

"Dad...?" I yanked on his arm, but he didn't respond. "Dad!"

He shook his head, snapping out of whatever trance he was in. He took me by the hand and squeezed hard. "Don't let go. You hear me? Don't let go."

I squeezed back with all my strength.

"Get ready to run," he whispered. I felt every muscle in his body tense, ready to spring into action. We stared at the tall shadow man creeping closer and closer.

I could see him, but at the same time I couldn't make out any details. He was a silhouette filled with dark emptiness. A starving void dragging us in, desperate to swallow us whole. A cold nothingness in the form of a person. The metallic grating of a rusted fork on a plate echoed in my head. I don't know how I knew, but it was coming from the shadow man. It sounded like he was laughing.

"Run!" Dad took off to the left, nearly pulling my arm from its socket. We raced through the woods. The laughter scratched at my eardrums. Branches and underbrush scraped my face and tore at my clothes trying to hold me back. The light of the setting sun struggled to reach us through the thickening trees, casting longer and darker shadows. I felt the shadow man's death rattle breathing just behind my ears, but I didn't dare turn around. We were running so fast that one slip, one errant step, and the looming darkness would have us.

My arm jerked back and Dad's hand ripped out of mine. Holding on for dear life, I didn't notice Dad had come to a complete stop. My feet flew out from under me, and I slammed hard into the dirt. Dad just stood there.

No, not standing. Hanging. Held aloft by a gaunt murky hand wrapped tight around his neck, the shadow man dangled Dad a few feet off the ground. He kicked and clawed at the vise grip, but it was no use.

I just stood there, frozen in absolute terror.

Dad locked eyes with me and choked out three words: "Run, Cody. Run!"

Then his head snapped to the side with a deep crunch. His hands fell limp. His legs stopped moving. The shadow man dropped Dad, and he fell to the ground in a heap. The laughter came back, louder and sharper than before.

Finally I ran. "Mom!" I cried with what little air I had left in my lungs. "*Mom!*" Tears streamed down my face. I ran as hard as I could through the blur of trees, branches, and bushes.

An arm wrapped around me and lifted me off the ground. I kicked and screamed, but it was useless. My whole body felt like jelly. I thought the shadow man had caught me.

"Cody!" Mom yelled. "Cody, what's wrong?"

I opened my eyes and saw my mom. I wrapped my arms around her, and a new wave of tears rushed down my cheeks. I could barely breathe. "Dad..." is all I got out.

She tried to hide the panic. "Cody, where's your father?"

I could only stare back to the woods, to the darkness, to where the shadow man waited.

"Stay here," she said as she got to her feet.

"*No*! You can't. The shadow man—"

She took me by the hand. "I have to find your father. If something's happened…"

I tried to hold her, but I had no strength left. She pulled away and headed into the woods. I stood there, trying to catch my breath, watching every dark corner of the forest. Seconds felt like forever. There was no sign of my mom. No sign of my dad. Nothing but me and the shadows.

The silence was shattered by a heartbreaking scream.

I tried to get to my feet, but another chill from behind knocked me to the ground. I turned to see the shadow man staring at me. Slow, deliberate, and as cold as the air around him, he waved goodbye. I couldn't tell, but I swear he was smiling. Then he slinked behind a tree and disappeared into the darkness.

All that was left was the rustling of the trees and the cries of my mom in the distance.

I blink away the memory and wipe the tear from the corner of my eye before it can fall. Once again on the couch in Dr. Hane's office, I make a conscious effort to stop my right leg from shaking. "We didn't know the woods got so dark so fast. We tried to hurry back, but we couldn't see where we were going. He must've tripped on a root or a rock or something and fell. When I found him…I ran to my mom."

Dr. Hane puts her pen down and takes off her glasses, looking me deep in the eyes, trying to read my every microexpression. "Is that what you believe? It was an accident? It wasn't your fault?"

"It wasn't my fault." This is the first true answer I've given her. My father's death wasn't my fault. It was Mr. Shadow's. I know because ever since that night, the dark spirit has never left my side.

I glance to my left, past the shelves with books and potted plants to the corner of the room. The only spot in the entire office with a hint of shadow. Standing there is the reason my father was dead. The black void that has haunted me for the last decade. A living nightmare. With his head crooked at an unnatural angle to fit just below the nine-foot ceiling, Mr. Shadow lifts a hollow hand and waves.

Chapter 2

Ten years, five months, and twenty-one days.

Frozen fingers claw at the base of my skull and scratch the back of my corneas as I stare at the red neon lights of my digital clock. 6:32 a.m. It's not the kind of cold you can hide from with a few extra blankets or a space heater. It's the kind that seeps into your soul and sits there, making all your muscles hurt. There's no open window or air conditioning to blame for the chill. I know it's coming from the closet. The closet that's open just a crack. The closet I made sure to close and lock last night before bed.

It's pitch-black, but I know *he's* in there staring back.

The twins shuffle in their bunk bed on the other side of the room. On top, Haylee lets out a soft groan. Below, Kaylee pulls the blankets closer. I can take the nightmares—I'm used to them—but it's not fair that they have to suffer too. They should be dreaming about riding horses and singing songs and play dates, not what *he* brings.

I toss the sheets aside and tiptoe over stuffed animals to the closet, but before I can wrap my fingers around the handle, the door creaks back and closes. I jerk it open only to find unicorn-printed shirts and glitter-bombed dresses hanging on rungs over a pile of mismatched socks next to way too many tiny shoes. No Mr. Shadow.

"Cody, what's wrong?" Kaylee rubs her tired eyes and props herself up on one elbow.

"It's nothing. Go back to sleep." She rolls over and is snoring in seconds.

The start of another wonderful Monday morning. I grab my clothes and head out of the room, but not before double-checking the closet to make sure Mr. Shadow is gone.

Ever since that day in the woods, he's been a perpetual darkness existing in my periphery, draining me like a dark parasite. I stopped playing sports because I was always exhausted from waking up screaming. I didn't want to hang out with my friends anymore because I was afraid of what Mr. Shadow would do to them. There was one day my mom convinced Jeffrey, my best friend in elementary school, to have a sleepover. He fell down the stairs and broke his arm. I know Mr. Shadow pushed him. I tried telling Mom about it, but she wouldn't or couldn't listen. She sent me to my first trauma specialist at eight years old. His diagnosis: my visions were a coping mechanism for the loss of my father.

I was ten when I was committed for the first time. Matthew Cosnic pushed me into a soccer goal post during P.E. Mr. Shadow fractured his leg in three places, but Matt and the school said I did it.

I bounced around from school to school, never lasting more than a year. Mom spent every dime she had trying to cure me. Specialists, hospitals, herbal remedies—she tried them all. But when I realized what all the stress and anxiety and fights were doing to my baby sisters, I stopped talking about it. It's my job as their big brother to protect them; if I had to suffer in silence alone so they could have a chance at being happy, so be it. So I bottled up the night terrors, the horrid visions, his invading darkness, and gave the answers my mom and her experts wanted to hear. But Mr. Shadow never left.

I still see light spirits, just not as many anymore. Too afraid of the predator that has staked his claim. The moment he shows up, they dart away like fish from a shark. A frigid chill and vanishing spirits let me know Mr. Shadow is near.

Now we live in Cedar Hills, California, in a small townhouse that has seen better days. There are cracks in the ceiling, moldy kitchen cabinets, and a funky smell coming from a discolored splotch in the living room carpet, just to name a few of its more endearing qualities. A recent house rule is no hot water while anyone is sleeping. The pipes creak and whine with winter right around the corner.

The first time I heard that sound, it triggered the hell out of me. When Haylee turned on the water, the pipes screamed so loud I thought Mr. Shadow had gotten her. No one appreciated me breaking down the door.

So instead of waking everyone up, I take a cold shower. Not my favorite part of the day, but I'll suffer the frigid water if it means some peace and quiet in the morning.

In vain I try to tame my short mop of wavy blond hair and change into a school uniform fitted for someone a few inches shorter and a few pounds heavier—a typical problem for a beanpole like me. My growth spurts started in middle school, so I've gotten used to clothes not fitting quite right. And it's not like we can afford new clothes every few months.

As I head to the kitchen, I'm greeted by the clattering of pots and pans opposite the small wooden island. A pair of worn heels poke out from under slacks wrapped in a fuzzy blue robe.

"Mom? What are you doing?"

On her hands and knees, she snaps around like a cornered cat. With her short hair pulled back tight, the blue robe over her white work shirt, and a lime green face mask, she looks like one of Kaylee's dolls that started melting. "Breakfast isn't going to make itself. I just can't find the scrambler. Scrambled eggs are easy. Oh…the toast. Can't forget the toast and the juice in the fridge. Oh, your tie's crooked."

I dodge her reach and head to the cupboard. "How about you save the micromanaging for the interview and finish getting ready?"

"I'm just so nervous, you know? We really need…" She doesn't have to finish; I've seen the overdue notifications.

We moved here because Mom landed a job as a teller at Cedar Hills Credit Union, and they've been interviewing prospective branch managers for the past month. It's the final round before they make their selection. Mom has the first slot at 8:00 a.m. sharp.

I pull a box of cereal out of the cupboard. "There. Breakfast handled."

"I'll give you and the girls some cash for lunch. Can you also drop them off? Oh, and before I leave…" She pulls a small pharmacy's worth of pills from her fuzzy pocket.

I don't even bother to groan anymore. There's no point. She's going to shove them down my throat whether I like it or not. Most are harmless: fish oils, essential vitamins, and such. The big one is Colesevelam, which balances my blood sugar. All so I can take my daily dose of Seroquel.

Seroquel is an antipsychotic medicine that changes the actions of chemicals in the brain and is used to treat schizophrenia in adults and children who are at least thirteen years old. I've read the bottle once or twice. This is our morning routine: I grab a glass of water, pop one pill at a time, swallow, then open wide and lift my tongue to prove I actually swallowed. Fish oils first, then vitamins, then the horse pill, and finally Seroquel.

I open my mouth on the last one and flip my tongue around like a dying fish. "You're going to be great at bossing everyone around."

"Thanks to seventeen years of training." Smirking, Mom heads to her room.

I wait for the audible click of the door closing before spitting out the Seroquel. I dry it off with a kitchen towel, slip it inside a Ziploc baggie with the rest of my weekend collection, and stuff the stash in the front zipper of my backpack.

I've stopped feeling bad about cheeking my meds. I used to feel guilty. Not because the doctors said I needed them, but because I didn't like lying to my mom. But after the last time she sent me away, I stopped caring how she felt. There was no hope of making her believe me.

Besides, I don't need them. I don't have schizophrenia. What I see is real. So instead I sell my meds to three stoners at school for twice the market value.

I throw together a couple of bowls of cereal for the girls while Mom finishes getting ready. As the milk hits the sugar balls, Haylee and Kaylee bound into the kitchen dressed in their matching uniforms and identical off-center ponytails. As if it wasn't already impossible to tell the two apart. They thrive on people mixing them up, especially Mom. The only noticeable difference to the untrained eye is the hint of a scar in the hairline of Kaylee's right temple from jumping on a motel bed, falling, and catching the corner of the nightstand. Mom stopped the bleeding with a butterfly bandage, but without stitches, Kaylee now has this little souvenir.

As the two inhale breakfast, I fix their ponytails with my best attempt at French braids.

Mom pokes her head around the corner, scrubbing the remnants of her green face mask off with a towel. "Cody's taking you two to school today. Mommy's got that important meeting. You listen to your brother, okay? You better hold his hand when crossing the street."

"Maybe if we got them those little leash backpacks, I could also teach them to sit."

Mom gives me the look only a worn-out single parent of three can have. It says. *I love you but if you screw up, I'll bury you alive in an unmarked grave.*

"I got them. Don't worry."

"Bye, Mommy. Good luck!" The twins wrap her in a warm embrace.

She kisses them both on top of their heads. "Thank you, my little rugrats. Now off you go. Don't want to be late for school."

With breakfast done and the bowls cleaned, I wrap the two in warm sweaters to hold back the fall's crisp bite and hurry the two out the door. I prefer walking to riding in Mom's car anyway. It's a rusted canary yellow four-door Civic that guzzles gas like a camel and squeals if you even think about touching the brakes. Not the best ride to roll up in to a private school where even the outcasts drive BMWs. Schools like this are quick to brand you for life, and I already have enough to work with being the new transfer.

It's not a bad walk either. Built back in the 1890s, Cedar Hills tried to keep a lot of the natural beauty. Instead of bulldozing everything and building over it, the town's roads wind with the flow of the land; houses are built between groupings of trees; and the parks are minimally maintained meadows. Out of all the places we've bounced around to, most of this one actually considers the environment.

But about ten minutes into the walk, there's a stark differentiation from our side of the street to the other. It's not gated per se, but I don't have to squint my eyes to see the line. They have a well-manicured bike path, hedges trimmed to perfection, and winding driveways that lead to unique two-story homes with stone or brick siding. On our side, the cars zoom right past the sidewalk; I almost get clipped by low-hanging branches; and cars are parked with half their bumpers on the sidewalk in front of cookie-cutter single stories. Even their half of the road has new asphalt with fresh paint to delineate sides.

This divide is just as obvious with the people. With a population of just over 1,800, in this town most residents on our side have lived in the same home generation after generation, keeping the history of this place alive and well. They run the mom-and-pop shops on Main Street, have periodic cul-de-sac potlucks, and wave from the porch on our walk to school.

Their side is made of artificially enhanced commuters tucked away behind a subtle wall of trees and planters. A twenty-minute drive in their next-gen electric cars from Silicon Valley, the tech and business moguls have chiseled out their little slice of heaven to get away from city life. And they've given the land an environmental facelift. Evergreen trees spaced equidistant from one another line the streets, creating an HOA-approved ratio of sunlight to shade. The slightest indication of a pothole is erased from existence in a matter of hours. Even the houses with their "vintage bones" have floor-to-ceiling windows and fiber internet.

At least my sisters have been informed that this is the place to go for pillowcases full of king-size candy bars on Halloween.

Another five minutes of walking and we reach Cedar Hill's crown jewel: North Creek Academy. This place does have a rod iron gate hidden under coiffed vines and hedges that encompasses the campus.

Nestled on the outskirts of Cedar Hills's famed forest, North Creek Academy is one of the top ten academic programs in the great state of California, or that's what they like to promote to every overbearing parent. The only reason we go here is because of their outreach program, which gives scholarships to families in need. For the application, I had to write an essay about "an obstacle in my life I had to overcome." I knew this school was the best chance my sisters had to get ahead in life and away from Mr. Shadow, so I wrote a sob story about learning to do a French braid for a play the girls were in since our mom was stuck at work. We got accepted.

Expensive cars of all shapes and sizes line up to deploy their kids, each fully accessorized in the latest designer trend. I stroll up with my accessories: Kaylee hanging from my neck and Haylee riding my left foot, both laughing their little heads off at their brother-shaped jungle gym. A few parents look down their professionally sculpted noses at us, but I don't care.

I drag my sisters to Head of Security Dave at the front gate. The stout man should audition for the Queen's

Guard. Not just because of his solemn expression but because most of the people that come to this school act like royalty.

"Hey, Dave. Dropping off Haylee and Kaylee Sterling."

Dave makes two quick checks.

"You hear about the teddy bear that broke into Ms. Bakers' Bakery? Guess he can't get enough of her blue bear-y pie either." Dave raises an eyebrow at me. "Yep, he was stuffed by the end. Bursting at the seams." The hint of a smile breaks through his hard exterior. Got him again. This man does love his dad jokes.

I reach into my pocket and turn to the twins. "For lunch today, Mom..." There's nothing but lint. Shit. Mom forgot again. "She gave us lunch money, which I'm going to hold on to. You two meet me here at noon and I'll give it to you then. Deal?"

"Deal!" the two shout back as they take off for their group of friends waving to them from their school's main doors.

With the twins dropped off, I pull out my phone and shoot a text off to Bryce, the stoner shot caller. *Sarah wants to meet. Now.*

I wave goodbye to Dave and head to the high school side of NCA.

Just like the other two high schools I've been to, the quad is divided into communities: jocks and cheerleaders get the shade under the three-hundred-year-old cedar in the center; gamers and nerds have the tables next to the science building; goths sit on the steps to the library, the burnouts and stoners hang out by the opposite fence behind the gym; and the overachievers flock from group to group. The rest are sprinkled about trying not to step too far into anyone's territory. Students may change, but the high school hierarchy will always be the same.

My phone buzzes. It's Bryce. *Can't wait to see her.*

As I bob and weave through the social landmines toward the football stadium, a glittering light catches my eye. A kaleidoscope of light spirits flows through the cedar tree: a thousand butterflies made of stained glass dance on the breeze. They drift closer, floating above the crowd of unaware students. I reach into my backpack to pull out my pencil and sketchbook, but before I can, the light spirits change course and dart over the building.

Cold creeps along my skin. Scanning the immediate area, I check all the dark recesses of the school and the woods just beyond it. That's where I spot him, unmoving in the forest: Mr. Shadow. Unlike the glimmering light spirits, his silhouette shudders with black static electricity.

"Yo, Codeine!" Bryce barks. Not the most flattering of nicknames, but what do you expect from a bunch of stoners when your name is Cody? He and his two buddies wait at the corner. "You introducing us or what?"

"Yeah…" I glance back to the woods, but Mr. Shadow is gone. "Be right there."

With more money dropped into it than most colleges, our football stadium is a mecca for man-children in plastic armor trying to impress scouts since their grades won't. Cedar Hills shuts down every Friday night to fill the stands up and cheer on the mighty Lions.

One of Bryce's followers, Jacob, is a prime example. Built like a wall and almost as smart, he's our starting linebacker. I'm pretty sure he had a full beard and could bench press me by the time he was twelve. D1 coaches come to their practices to watch this guy.

The other lanky string of frayed nerves is Scotty. His head is always on a swivel, twitching back and forth like a prairie dog hopped up on Adderall. If his parents hadn't made a sizable donation every semester, the school would've expelled him freshman year.

Then there's Bryce. He puts on a devil-may-care show everyone falls for. Just enough bedhead to make it look like he doesn't try. Tie undone to catch the ire of his teachers, but not enough to do something about it. It's his eyes, however, that have always unsettled me. They remind me of Mr. Shadow: black and empty. When Bryce stares at me, it feels like I don't even exist to him.

At the end of the day, though, we need the money, and they have plenty of it.

I head through the tunnel that leads to the immaculate field and dip under the stadium seating. Bryce, Jacob, and Scotty are waiting.

I pull out my Seroquel stash. "With the quick turnaround, this is all I got, so you owe me—"

"Nothing," Bryce finishes. He flashes me an empty smile. "I did a little math. Looks like you've been making quite a pretty penny on our account." With a nod, his two flunkies move to either side of me.

A chill slithers from the base of my skull and down my spine. My mouth flash dries and I can't get a full breath. As unnerving as Bryce's dead eyes are, there's only one thing that can elicit such a primeval flight reaction in me.

Not good. Really not good. "That's capitalism for you." I try to hide the panic in my voice. "I got the supply; you got the demand."

Bryce moves forward and I take an involuntary step back, finding myself pressed against a concrete wall. "Well, we have a new demand: free. I don't like being taken advantage of, Codeine. It hurts my feelings."

I hear him first. The voice sounds like Bryce, but it's twisted. The sound makes my teeth ache, like an angle grinder cutting sheet metal.

Here, kitty, kitty, kitty. I'm not gonna hurt you...

Please, not now... But Mr. Shadow never listens. He keeps whispering, telling me things I shouldn't know, showing me things I shouldn't see. People's deepest, darkest secrets. Memories they want to keep buried. But Mr. Shadow knows it all and he tells me everything.

The aluminum stairs fade away, replaced by aged shiplap walls, a door with a cartoonish goat head painting, and rows of overflowing trash bins. I'm not at school—I'm in the back alley behind the town's only dive bar: the Thirsty Goat. And there's Bryce, kneeling a few feet from an orange tabby cat with a neon-green collar, offering an opened can of tuna fish.

The first time Mr. Shadow did this, I was twelve. I thought I was imagining things. I saw an old neighbor of ours beat his daughter with a dictionary. When she was taken away, I was too young to put two and two together. A few months later, I saw the PTA president at a school in Bend, Oregon pour rat poison into the marinara sauce and serve it to her husband. When the police arrested her, I realized what Mr. Shadow was doing.

It's happened again and again: normal-looking people doing terrible things.

And now Bryce and the cat. There's no use yelling or trying to stop it. I've tried. I'm not really there. All I can do is watch the cat come closer, desperate for a bite of food. Watch Bryce grab an ebony-handled switchblade with a silver snakehead engraving in his back pocket...

Another flash. I'm in a marble-floored six-car garage. Bryce lifts the air duct grating above the electric double doors and pulls out a stainless steel box. He opens it and drops a bloodied neon-green collar onto a pile of others.

"Earth to Codeine. Come in, Codeine." The present flashes back with Bryce an arm's length away, his black pupils staring through me.

Scotty and Jacob have closed in as well; I'm cornered. "How about I hook you guys up with a discount? Three for the price of one." That's at least enough to cover Haylee and Kaylee for lunch.

"I think I'm going to take a little more than that." Bryce whips out his ebony-handled switchblade with a silver snakehead engraving.

Every muscle locks. I choke on the scream stuck in my throat. I try to run, but I'm frozen, staring at the tall dark silhouette looming behind them.

Jacob is first. Mr. Shadow lifts him off the ground with ease. There's confusion on the athlete's face, trying to rationalize how he's levitating. Just as the fear sets in, Mr. Shadow hurls the kid against the backside of the stairway. His skull cracks against the metal, and he falls to the ground in a still heap, leaving a splash of blood on the dented step.

My mind races back a decade. To the woods. To the first time I felt the cold.

Scotty screams. Warm droplets spatter my face.

Dad's hand rips from my grip.

Bones break. A knife clatters to the ground. I blink and see Bryce's hand, his fingers bent in the wrong direction. As he cries in agony, Mr. Shadow twists both his elbows back farther and farther until they snap.

My dad collapses in the dirt, but his face is twisted 180 degrees to stare at me. His mouth wide-open. More bones break, the snap echoing from inside Dad's dark maw. Again and again and again. I just stand there, helpless.

Chapter 3

I'm numb. I can't feel the tanned leather chair I'm sitting in, the police-issue wool blanket wrapped around me, or the NCA gym shirt they gave me after mine was taken as evidence. Apparently, it had blood spatter on it. Maybe Scotty's?

It's all been a blur. Head of Security Dave helping me through the crowd, medics checking my condition, police taking pictures and questioning me...

Now I'm in the dean's office, flanked by two uniformed officers, watching Dean Aldrich pace behind his desk, mumbling about a response team and how to manage this PR nightmare.

The last time I was this triggered, my psychiatrist had me focus on the small details around me. I start with the rich mahogany desk and matching bookshelves, polished to the point where I can see my reflection. I imagine with the putting-green carpet there are a few clubs hidden behind his rows and rows of books. There's no way he's read all these; some have to be fake.

Dean Aldrich looks like a guy with fake books: overweight with a shiny bald head, salt-and-pepper goatee, and snarky eyes behind perfectly round wired glasses. He adjusts his plaid jacket with brown elbow patches before sitting back behind his desk. He just needs an old school smoking pipe and the smug fraud look would be complete.

A screech I'm all too familiar with, one that brings relief and terror, cuts through the awkward silence. Outside the window, a rusted canary-yellow four-door Civic skids to a stop on the curb, and my mom rushes out. I've seen that look on her face before and God help anyone who gets in her way.

It takes my mom only a few seconds before she barges in like a raging grizzly with an officer on her tail.

"Ma'am, you can't go in there. I'm sorry, sir. She just—"

"Who the hell wants to explain to me why my son is being detained in a room with a bunch of grown-ass men asking him questions without his legal guardian here?" Her brown eyes flash back and forth from the officers to the dean, daring one of them to challenge her.

Aldrich steps on the hornet's nest. "Ms. Sterling, my name's Dean Aldrich. Your son—"

"I don't give a damn who you are! You *cannot* treat my son like this. After what he just went through? You should be ashamed of yourself." She turns to me, and in that split second, the rage disappears. "You okay?"

I just watched Mr. Shadow fold a classmate like origami. I can still feel blood on my cheek. "Yeah. I'm fine."

That terrifying visage crosses her face again. She turns to the nearest officer, who takes a step back. "Is my son under arrest?"

"Not at the moment, ma'am, but—"

"Cody's on medication, correct?" Dean Aldrich interjects. He holds up a manila folder with "Sterling, Cody" written on the tab. "A young man with his condition, two little sisters, and growing up in a single-parent household—it makes for a dangerous concoction. With no father figure, I'm surprised—"

Before either the cops or Dave can react, Mom lunges for the dean. He shrinks back, pinned between the wall and his desk. She jerks the manila folder from his grasp. "Screw your file and screw you! My son is a good kid, you hear me? And if you ever question my capabilities as a mother again, I swear I will feed you your own beating heart."

Mom throws the folder at the dean, scattering papers across his table. She turns back, takes me by the arm, and storms out of the room.

Aldrich's voice echoes down the hall after us. "Your son is suspended until further notice, and we will be reevaluating those scholarships!"

Without saying another word, my mom drags me through the halls, down the stairs, out the front doors, and into the car.

Haylee and Kaylee sit in the backseat, their hands in their laps, unmoving. Mom must have grabbed them before she came to get me. She jams the key in the ignition, turns the engine over, and rips out of the gravel parking lot.

The twins know better than to say anything, but I have to risk it; I have to explain myself. My mom needs to know I didn't do this. I need her to believe me. I open my mouth, but the words get caught in my throat when my eyes fall on the digital clock on the center console: 8:17 a.m. Mom's interview started seventeen minutes ago.

This must be how death-row inmates feel when they're marched to the chair. No one speaks. No one even moves until we pull into the driveway. Haylee, Kaylee, and I hold our collective breath and wait.

Mom's calm is disturbing. "Haylee, Kaylee, go to your room. I need to talk to Cody."

Telling my sisters to go to their room is like trying to get a Jack Russell terrier to sit still for a bath. They go stir crazy and will be building forts with the mattresses and hanging from the bed frames if unsupervised for more than five minutes. But this time they know better. Both of them race into the house without a single complaint.

Mom steps out and doesn't even turn back when she goes inside. I've seen her mad before, but this is a whole new level.

I take a deep breath, pray it isn't my last, and start the long walk to meet my maker... literally. I open the door and see her waiting in the kitchen.

Before I get a word out, she holds up a small plastic cup. "Pee. Now." It's a drug test cup. Back in the psych ward, they made us piss in them to see what sort of drugs or meds were in our system. She hasn't asked me to pee in one for almost a year now. "I'm not asking."

Shit. I can't. The problem isn't what's in my system—it's what isn't. "I can explain–"

Mom hurls the cup at me. "Goddamn it, Cody! Are you kidding me? How long, huh? How long have you been off your meds?!"

I freeze. She's never screamed at me like this, never even raised a hand. "I-I…"

"What have you been doing with your pills? Are you flushing them? Do you know how expensive they are? I can barely keep food on the table and you're throwing them away!"

"No, I'm not!" I snap back at the accusation. "Those guys pay twice as much. You forgot lunch money again, so I was—"

"You're selling them? Holy shit, Cody—you're a drug dealer?!"

"It's not like that. You said we need the money. I'm just trying to help."

"By selling your meds?! Are you crazy?" As she says it, she freezes. "You're not on your meds… Cody, what happened today? What happened between you and those boys?"

"I'm not crazy. It wasn't me. I swear I didn't do anything."

"I heard the police," she says. "No one else was in there. It was just you and—"

"It was Mr. Shadow!" I couldn't keep it back. I had to tell her. She has to understand. Once the word vomit starts, there's no stopping it. "Bryce wasn't going to pay. They said because I overcharged, they wanted it all for free. They cornered me in the stadium. That's when Mr. Shadow came. He was whispering to me, showing me what Bryce did to those pets. He keeps their collars as trophies in the air vent in the garage. Mr. Shadow attacked them, not me!" I stop to catch my breath.

My mother just stands there, slack-jawed, staring at me like she doesn't know who I am.

"Mom, say something. Please." I take a step closer, but she jumps back and puts up a defensive hand. "Please. You have to believe—"

"I don't want to hear this. Cody, what have you done?"

"But Mr. Shadow—"

"Isn't real!" she explodes. "Jesus Christ, you've been lying to me for God knows how long. I thought we had something good going. I trusted you! And now—you haven't been taking your meds; you're selling them; and you nearly beat three classmates to death. Do you even know what it's like for me? What I have to do just to keep this roof over your head? You have no clue! The second I get an opportunity, you go and screw it all up. You've taken everything from me—what more do you want?"

"I've taken *everything*?" I snap. "Really? When was the last time I got to be a normal teenager? Who makes Haylee and Kaylee breakfast and lunch and takes them to school? Who helps them with their homework and does their hair and everything else a parent should do? Me. I have to 'cause you're never around. Never!"

"Cody—"

"I hate you! Dad believed me. I wish you died instead of him!"

The moment it leaves my mouth, I know it's wrong, but I want to hurt her, make her feel the same way I feel. I don't apologize. Instead I run to my room and slam the door behind me. Haylee and Kaylee are there, sitting on the bottom bunk.

"You okay, Cody?" Haylee whispers.

"Get out!"

The two sprint out. I wait, expecting my mom to charge in for yelling at my sisters, to continue our fight, to scream things back at me, but no one comes through the door.

I'm not crazy! I know I didn't do this. It was Mr. Shadow. It's all his fault.

I tried to be good. To be what she wanted. I really did, and I thought we were better. Ever since I was diagnosed, she looked at me differently. Like I was a freak. But when they put me on those meds, she started seeing me like I was her son again. She treated me like I was normal and not something made of glass that could shatter if not handled carefully.

But that was all a lie and I fell for it.

Chapter 4

That night, Mom had the twins sleep in her room. I thought it would be great to finally have the room to myself, but I felt more like a prisoner than anything else. The only interaction I had with my warden was a knock on my door. When I opened it, I found dinner served on a tray on the floor.

Even Mr. Shadow had left me alone. I guess he figured he'd done enough damage for one day, but I still couldn't sleep. After a decade of my having my sisters as roommates, the silence was deafening.

This morning, when hunger finally drove me from my cell, Mom had already taken Haylee and Kaylee to school. I was home alone. Any teen's dream, right? Not when I'm waiting for the police to break down the door and take me away for attempted murder, or for Mom to come home from work... I'd rather face the police.

I spent most of the day commuting from the couch to the fridge and back with a periodic detour to the bathroom. By the time my sisters got home from school, I was actually relieved to have some human interaction.

The front door flies open and the two charge in like mini tornadoes. "Cody! You're famous!" they cry out in unison. Seriously, that twin thing is real.

Before I even begin to find out what they're talking about, I watch the door. Mom should be right behind them, but Kaylee locks it.

"Where's Mom?"

"Mrs. Davis dropped us off," Haylee replies.

Weird but not uncommon. When Mom works late, she has our neighbor, Mrs. Davis, drive us. But usually it's on rainy days, and Mom gives me a heads-up. I guess since we're not talking and I'm suspended from school, it makes sense.

"Everyone's talking about you," Kaylee says as the two drag me to the living room couch. "They're saying you went crazy and beat up those guys with a football."

"No, Patricia said he used his psychic abilities."

"I heard Savannah say Cody's a witch and summoned a demon to—"

"Okay, that's enough." Fantastic, there goes any hope of a normal reputation. I knew the high school rumor mill was going to be crazy but hitting the elementary side in less than twenty-four hours must be a new record. Also, the demon thing isn't exactly wrong... "You two know I didn't do anything, right?"

The two nod. "Duh. You didn't even squish that spider that was crawling over my bed," Kaylee points out.

"And we can beat you up," Haylee follows.

"Oh, yeah? I'd like to see you try!" I lunge forward and tickle any spot I can reach. They burst into fits of hysterical laughter as they struggle to escape.

I relent when their faces turn a light purple. The two lay there, trying to catch their breaths. Then Kaylee sits up with a bright smile on her face. "Can we build a fort in the room?"

"Yay!" adds Haylee. "It's not a school night."

"Please, please, pleasepleaseplease," the two shout.

"Fine." I feign reluctance, but with the anxious day I've had, a little make-believe sounds fun. "But I get to pick the name this time."

An hour later, our whole bedroom has been turned into Castle Awesome Unicorn. I was outvoted. Chairs line up to create crawlspace hallways; mattresses are cushioned walls; and draped pink blanket ceilings make the foundation of our little castle. Haylee and Kaylee even have their stuffed animals working as cooks, maids, and butlers in their designated rooms.

"Let's play Hot/Cold," Haylee announces as her stuffed bear finishes making our spaghetti and rainbow confetti pasta.

Kaylee stops helping the plastic show ponies clear the vampire bats from the dungeon. "We go first. Close your eyes, Cody!"

I oblige. I have no idea why, but Hot/Cold is the twins' favorite game. The rules are simple: they take something of mine, hide it, and I have to find it. I get to ask if I'm hotter or colder to the hiding spot five times. If

I'm getting closer, they tell me hotter. If I'm moving in the wrong direction, I get colder. If I find it within ten seconds after the last question, I win.

"Okay, open your eyes!" Haylee and Kaylee sit in the middle of the fort wearing sneaky smiles. "You have to find the shell."

The shell is a small white spiky conch with a dull pink opening we found last year during a sunny daddy/daughter beach day back in Oregon. Since Mom was busy with work, I volunteered to take them. The girls spent most of the day playing in the water with their friends while I hid in a beach chair under an umbrella. At one point they dragged me to the water to at least get my feet wet. As the ice-cold waves lapped over my bare feet, a school of guppy light spirits swam around my legs.

As I watched the creatures glide in the ebb and flow of the water and listened to my sisters laugh with their friends, I imagined walking out into the ocean. Go until my head dipped below the waves and never resurface.

I could finally be rid of Mr. Shadow.

I could be free.

A heartbeat later, I forced the ideation from my mind. I couldn't do that to my family. To my sisters. Without me, what would Mr. Shadow do to them? Would I be condemning them to a lifetime of pain and suffering?

That's when the guppy spirits darted back into the ocean. A deep chill in the back of my lungs made the frigid ocean feel like a spa. I needed to find Haylee and Kaylee. The twins were in a small group of girls jumping over the waves about fifty yards down the beach. Farther out into the deep blue waters, a large wave manifested with a dark figure in the heart of the rising surge. I called for the girls to come in, but they either couldn't hear me or ignored me. I took off running, but the wet sand dragged my feet down. Mr. Shadow's inky black silhouette shifted with the approaching wave, his head turning from me to Haylee and Kaylee. I dove into the water, but I knew I wouldn't make it.

I watched all the girls jump over the wave, except Haylee; the demonic wave swallowed her. I swam as fast as I could, trying to yell for Kaylee to find her sister but kept breathing in lungfuls of salt water. I was too far away. How would I explain this to Mom?

Then Haylee popped up a few feet from me with the seashell in her hands. She had stepped on it while jumping over the previous wave and wanted to see what it was. She and her sister were all smiles since I decided to come out and play with them.

The unholy mirage of Mr. Shadow watched from shore. I got the message loud and clear: he could take my sisters whenever and wherever, and there was nothing I could do about it. Don't ever think about leaving him again.

To the girls, the shell is a wonderful day at the beach with their big brother. To me, it's a threat, a warning, a promise that if I ever step out of line, my sisters will pay the price.

I scan our castle for anything that seems out of place, but after years of playing this game, the girls have gotten adept at hiding their trail. I know it took only seconds to hide the shell, so at least they didn't leave this room.

I scoot forward just one step. "Hotter or colder?"

"Hotter! Four more." They love to count down the questions.

Okay, so that eliminates the half behind me. I move to my right. "Hotter or colder?"

"Colder! Three more times."

So it's in the upper-left quadrant. That means the shell could be in our makeshift ballroom, library, or horse stable. Kaylee is giggling a little more than usual, and she's in front of the stables, so I head to the left. "Hotter or colder?"

"Colder. Two more to go!"

Damn, her giggle was a red herring. That leaves the library and the ballroom. If I go to the library in the middle, they'll say "hot" no matter what. So I work my way over to the ballroom on the far right. "Hotter or colder?"

"Colder. Last one!"

The library it is. Pillows stack side by side against the far mattress wall. Haylee has one of her stuffed triceratopses facedown, reading one of her imaginary books.

I move to the shelf of pillow books. "Hotter or colder?"

"Colder! That's five questions. Ten, nine, eight—"

Screeching brakes signal Mom's arrival. My heart plummets. Guess pretending everything is okay can only last so long. Out the castle window, she gets out of her car, anxiously digging a thumb into the palm of her hand. A large unmarked white van parks behind her, the type parents warn their kids to stay away from because there are no puppies or candy inside. Two men step out.

One is a tall, thin, middle-aged man with a buzz cut failing to hide a receding hairline wearing a green plaid dress shirt with sleeves rolled up to highlight the tattoos running the length of both arms, worn jeans, and a pair of light brown felt sneakers. Next to him is a rotund guy about the same age but a head shorter with a salt-and-pepper crew cut and thick chinstrap beard framing his big smile, a brick-red business casual sweater over his dress shirt, gray dress pants, and matching loafers.

Mom leads them into the house. They're too casual to be the police, but her nervous body language sends all the warning bells in my head into overdrive.

"Three, two, one—"

I flip over the pillow with the stuffed triceratops, revealing the seashell.

"Ugh!" The twins groan. "Every time. How are you so good?"

"Cody, can you come to the living room please?" Mom calls out.

I hand the twins the shell. "You two stay here and find another place to hide this. I'll be back in a minute." The two brainstorm as I leave.

I find the two men from the creepy van waiting in the living room and Mom pouring four glasses of water.

The lanky one gives me a friendly smile and waves me over. "Hey there, my man. You must be Cody.

Name's Jeremy. Nice to meet you." He reaches out a hand. I cross my arms. "This is my colleague, Steve."

Steve ushers me over to the couch. "You mind grabbing a seat so we can talk?"

I stay put. I glance at my mom, but she focuses on the glasses.

Jeremy leans forward. "I hear you're having some problems at home and school. Things getting a little out of control? Your mom gave us a call and asked if we could help."

"Help? What kinda help? Who are you guys?" This really isn't good.

"We're from New Beginnings," Steve answers. "We're a non-profit that helps teens like you get away from the chaos of their lives for a while and give them the opportunity to face their challenges head-on. Our clinical psychologists are some of the best in the—"

"You're sending me away?!" I turn on my mom. I know what this is. Mom used to threaten me with it. It's like a psych ward you live at for months. No phone, no internet, just a bunch of other crazy kids dealing with their issues twenty-four-seven. I never thought she'd actually follow through. "But I didn't do anything wrong."

I see tears welling in her eyes, but I don't care. She betrayed me...again! She keeps her attention on her glass of water. "This is for your own good."

"How would you know what's good for me? You don't care! You don't even believe me."

Jeremy shifts forward in his chair. "Listen, dude, we wouldn't be here if your mom didn't love you. I know it's hard to see that now. I totally get it—you feel ganged up on. I mean, you got two strange guys in your house telling you they're taking you away. I freaked out when that happened to me too. But I promise you, we're only here to help. You just want someone to hear you, to believe you? That's what we do, my man."

"Believe me?" I snap. "If my mother believed me, you wouldn't be here."

"You left me no choice," Mom counters. "You pull this crap when you're an adult and they won't suspend you, they'll send you to jail."

Steve cuts in before I can respond. "New Beginnings is in the Payette National Forest just outside of McCall, Idaho. The idea is to get you back to the basics. Help you discover the person you want to be. We supply you with all the necessary equipment to live comfortably out there: a tent, sleeping bag, clothing, et cetera so you don't need to pack anything. Think of it like an extended camping trip, but where you get to process a lot of what you're going through."

My heart pounds in my ears. My lungs crash against my chest so hard it feels like I'm going to pass out. Their voices fade away.

The woods. She's sending me to the woods. Trees flash in my mind. Shadows stretching, growing taller. Dad and me running. Mr. Shadow laughing. Dad lifted off the ground.

Steve rests a gentle yet firm hand on my shoulder. "Hey buddy, I need you to calm down. Okay? It's not that bad—"

"You're sending me to the freaking woods?!" I scream at Mom. "Are you kidding me?"

"They say it's the best one for you. That being out there will help—"

"Send me to jail—I don't care. There's no way I'm going to the goddamn woods."

Jeremy shakes his head. "This isn't an option, my man. We're here to pick you up and help you be okay with that. But we're going, one way or another. We just really prefer the one where you choose to go."

All the air is sucked out of the room. How could this be happening? I didn't do anything! It was Mr. Shadow. It's always been Mr. Shadow. But I'm the one who's getting taken away.

Mom wipes a tear from her face. "Please, Cody, think of your sisters. You have to do this. You have to get better. If not for me, do it for them."

"Don't you dare use them like that," I force through a quivering jaw. I feel cold and empty, except this time it's not because of Mr. Shadow. It's because of *her*. I want to fight, to argue, to scream—anything that would help convince them to leave me here—but the truth is this is happening. I'm going to the wilderness. And it's all Mom's fault. "Can I at least say goodbye to Haylee and Kaylee?"

"I don't know if that's such a—" Mom starts.

"You got a minute," Steve interrupts. Mom shoots him a look, but he waves her off.

As I head back to the room, I hear Jeremy whisper to my mom, "Only way this is going to work is if he trusts us, and I've learned with kids like your son, trust is earned."

I step into Castle Awesome Unicorn and find my sisters waiting in the center. "There's no way you'll find your shoe this time, Cody," Haylee challenges.

Kaylee nods. "Yeah, this one's—"

"We're going to have to pause the game," I cut in. "I have to go away for a little while."

"What? No!" Haylee cries. "You said you didn't do anything wrong."

"It's not a bad thing. It's like a sleepaway camp for big kids." I could run and disappear. Get away from Jeremy and Steve and New Beginnings, away from North Creek Academy, away from Mom...

Kaylee is near tears. "I don't want you to go."

But I can't abandon them. "I know, but I have to," I pull them in and squeeze them as hard as I can. "I love you two so much."

A minute later, Mom's waiting by the front door with my sketchbook and a pen in hand.

"They said you can have one personal item. They were very specific about the limitations. I hope I made the right choice..." Tears build in her eyes.

I bite my tongue and take the single permitted personal item. No matter the rage and pain warring inside me, I'll leave with dignity. I need to be strong for Haylee and Kaylee.

But as I step outside, Mom adds, "Please tell me I made the right choice."

Any semblance of emotional control is shattered with the plea. Like a cornered rattlesnake, I turn on her and lash out with venomous vitriol. "You're getting rid of me and want *me* to make *you* feel better? That's not happening. What you're doing… This isn't love. This is abandonment. You've given up on me. You're sending me to suffer while you finally get to live your normal life. I hope you're happy. Just so you know, I'll never forgive you for this."

Leaving her stunned and wounded, I head for the van. But as Steve slides the door open, the twins try to rush past Mom. "Don't go, Cody! Please!"

With one foot in the vehicle, I hesitate. Every fiber of my being wants to charge back into that house and hide in Castle Awesome Unicorn with the two of them for the rest of my life. For all I know, this is a potential death sentence. But if I go, so does Mr. Shadow. Haylee and Kaylee will be safe. No more nightmares. No more suffering. They can be normal.

Steve walks up next to me. "This is the hardest part. Just remember, this is for them."

I get in the back and wave goodbye as they slide the door shut. Mom, cheeks streaked with tears, struggles to hold my sisters back. With a jerk, the van starts down the street, and all I can do is watch my world shrink and disappear out the back window.

Chapter 5

For the next seven hours, Jeremy and Steve try to convince me that everything is going to be okay, that I'm making the right choice, and that it's not as bad as I think it's going to be, but it all goes in one ear and out the other. I'm lost in my mind, replaying all the times Mr. Shadow ruined my life. Anytime I'd start to make a friend, he found a way to push them away. I was his toy to play with; no one else's. And now he's taken my family too.

The van comes to a stop, jolting me from the dark rabbit hole. Pins and needles shoot through my stiff muscles. The sun has dropped low over the horizon, almost touching the evergreen treetops. Behind us, the road is a long stretch of absolutely nothing.

Outside my window, a bright-red neon sign sitting atop a restaurant catches my attention: *Shelly's Diner*. Turquoise paneling with a checkered racing stripe wrapping around the middle sparkles along the side of the retro building. There's even a neon-blue analog clock sitting above the double-door entrance. And it's all pristine, as if I've been teleported to the 1950s.

Jeremy hops out. "Welcome to Idaho, my man. This is your last chance to get a bite of a delicious greasy burger and use a real toilet for the next couple of months. I recommend you take advantage of both. Plus, you'll get a chance to meet Shelly. She's something else."

"You just like her 'cause she gives you free pie," Steve jokes as he opens the sliding door and escorts me in.

The inside has the classic hot rod red leather booths and checkerboard tiled floor, but the decor looks like a grandmother's garage sale threw up all over the place. Christmas lights zigzag across the ceiling; rosy-cheeked lawn gnome lamps mark the center of each table; paintings of surfing ferrets and dancing pandas decorate the walls; and a massive stuffed alligator with a sombrero hangs over the bar.

A petite waitress about my age with perfect posture waits behind the pink-and-green palm tree host stand. For how zany this oasis of tacky is, she's the opposite. The part down the middle of her shoulder-length auburn hair would make a ruler jealous and the tacky buttons on her old-school diner suspenders are level and equally spaced. Even her candy-striped uniform is ironed.

Her anxious hands betray the calm facade. They dart from her side, to interlocked on the host stand, to stacking the menus, to arms crossed, then back to her sides.

She nudges her thin, tortoiseshell, green rectangular glasses up a little with her index finger and flashes a practiced smile. "Hello and welcome to Sherry's Diner." Even her greeting sounds like a how-to guide. "My name is Nessy. How many?"

"Hot diggity, look at what the cat dragged in!" A pudgy lady with short spiked gray hair and red flamingo sunglasses sits behind a counter decorated with antlers. She spots us and her face lights up. "If it isn't my favorite tall drink of water and spicy tuna. How are you boys doing?" She nods toward me. "Still saving the world, one lost soul at a time I see."

Jeremy pulls up a seat at the counter. "Hey, Shelly. When did you start hiring?"

"First day on the job, bless her heart. Sweet girl and smart as a whip, but stiffer than my Long Island special. Then Chester goes and gets some flu, so I had to call in a new cook too. Guy's got chops—I'll give him that. Makes a burger that'll blow those taste buds outta your face."

"It's all about the secret ingredient," a baritone voice chimes in. A bald head with a bright smile that stands in stark contrast to his dark skin pops up in the kitchen. The human mountain almost fills the entire window, and he has to lean on the counter to see us. His spotless white apron is about to explode at the seams. Even the guy's muscles have muscles. He holds up a handle of bourbon that disappears in his grip and gives me a wink. "Don't worry, kiddo. It cooks out."

Steve sits me down between him and Jeremy. "Not tonight. Shelly, please tell me you still have that rhubarb pie. I've been craving it for weeks."

"Anything for you, sweetheart. And you like your eggs running out the door?"

"You know it." Steve nods. "And some black coffee when you get a chance."

"Done. And how about for…" Shelly hesitates, peering at me from behind her crazy glasses. "My, oh my, what have we here?"

"Easy there, Shelly." Steve chuckles. "Don't want you making Jeremy jealous now. Let's get the young man your famous Shelly burger and a soda."

But Shelly ignores Steve. "I haven't seen someone like you in a long time. Dying breed. Pity if you ask me. The world is such a strange and beautiful place, wouldn't you agree?"

She pulls her sunglasses down the bridge of her nose to reveal her electric-blue eyes. Eyes just like mine. She gives me a quick wink before hiding them behind the flamingos again.

"I'll get that going for you boys right away," and before I can ask Shelly a single question, she turns and disappears behind the swinging doors.

Jeremy shakes his head. "Told you she was something else. We met her years ago…"

I'm not listening. I'm staring at the swinging doors. Or rather, what sauntered through them. A feline light spirit with long, floppy rabbit ears. It leaps onto the bar and finds a comfortable spot under a set of heat lamps and makes a sound that's a blend between a purr and the rustling of long grass in a gentle breeze.

I take a good look around the diner and notice the light spirit wasn't the only one. Small sparrow-like ones dart around the ceiling while a few ferrets curl up on the empty couches. The diner is bustling with them.

I've never seen anything like this before. The warmth radiating from all the creatures in such a tight space feels like a cozy fire on a snowy day. For the first time in what feels like days, I catch myself smiling. The positive energy is intoxicating.

A spotted golden retriever with ram horns strolls over and takes a seat next to me. With a slight huff, it rests its head on my knee, making my leg tingle. It takes all my self-control not to try and scratch it behind the horns. Steve and Jeremy already think I'm crazy; I don't need them seeing me petting thin air.

The happy light spirits seem at peace here.

With a wink, Shelly slides a burger in front of me. "Making friends already. That's Luna. She's my favorite, but don't tell the others. They come from all over. Really brings some life to the place, don't you think?"

A bolt of electricity surges through my body, short-circuiting me. My muscles lock in place, my breathing stops, and my jaw opens and closes like a robotic goldfish with no sound coming out. For all I know, my heart has stopped too. I can only stare at this eccentric old lady in absolute shock and awe with the simple and world-altering realization: she can see spirits too.

"Luna?" Steve eavesdrops.

Shelly gives me a pat on the back of my numb hand and grabs our order from the kitchen window. She plops a plate of runny eggs and coffee in front of Steve and a healthy slice of pie for Jeremy.

The plate is barely on the table before Jeremy impales his dessert with a fork. His eyes almost roll into the back of his head. "Oh, Shelly, you are incredible."

He doesn't know the half of it. I can still feel the warm tingle of the now snoring spirit dog on my leg. "You… You can really see—"

Shelly gives a quick shake of her head and glances at my two escorts. Both are focused more on their food than us, but she still leans in and whispers. "Best if you keep this your little secret. Don't want people thinking you're crazy."

Too late.

Steve glances at his watch mid-bite. "Shoot. We're late. Shawn's going to kill us." He turns to Shelly. "Can we take this on the road? Don't want to leave the boss lady waiting."

Shelly grabs some to-go boxes from the counter and loads the leftovers. The bunny cat nuzzles against the back of her hand, and she gives it a quick scratch behind its ears. To anyone else watching, it would seem like an old lady stretching her tired fingers.

Steve hurries us out the door. "Sorry to rush, Shelly. You know how Shawn can get."

Shelly walks us out. "Don't you worry 'bout a thing. You boys just drive safe and—" She stops in her tracks as all the light spirits dart into the café.

The night air fills with the noxiously sweet aroma of ozone, and a cold spider crawls in the pit of my stomach. For a split second I'm relieved. There was a nagging whisper in the back of my mind since I left home. What if Mr. Shadow doesn't follow? What if my waking nightmare stays to torture my family? What if I've left them to the devices of a monster they can't see? But the cold fear gripping my chest alleviates those concerns.

Just visible in the glow of the neon sign, I spot the menacing nightmare staring at me from the fringe of the woods like a hungry lion waiting in the tall underbrush. Mr. Shadow stands there, a static void against the dark forest. His head tilts with a demented curiosity to one side farther and farther until it seems to pop perpendicular to his shoulders.

Shelly puts a protective arm between me and Mr. Shadow, her eyes locked on the evil entity watching from a few dozen yards away. But her electric-blue eyes aren't filled with dread. They glare back with a fierceness I didn't know the sweet woman was capable of.

"You can see him too?" I whisper to her.

Shelly turns her intense glare on me and pulls me close. "Listen, my dear, you can't be afraid. Spectrals are drawn to powerful energies. They feed on it. But the dark ones—like that—thrive on pain and fear. You must be strong. Stronger than you can imagine. The world is full of great and terrible things; you must believe in yourself."

"Let's go," Jeremy calls from the van. "Don't want to start at New Beginnings on the wrong foot."

"But… You can… How?" I stammer, desperate to hold on to this remarkable stranger. I've been in the dark for more than a decade, haunted by the demonic presence that took my father, and suddenly there's a beacon of hope. A light in the darkness. It's so jarring, I don't know what to say. I have so many questions, but I don't know where to start. How does she know so much about…spectrals? What are they? Where do they come from? Has she always been able to see them? Why can't anyone else? Are there others like us?

But before I can find the words, Steve's hand falls on my shoulder. "Sorry to break up the party, but we really have to get going. Thank you again, Shelly."

She gives me a reassuring nod. "You can do this."

As Steve herds me into the van, I hazard one more glance at the woods, but Mr. Shadow has vanished. Shelly, with her spiked gray hair and electric-blue eyes hidden behind flamingo glasses, waves goodbye from under the bright lights as Jeremy puts the van in gear.

With a lurch, we take off down the road, leaving behind the one person in this world who truly understands what I'm going through. As much as I want to jump out and never leave that colorful diner, I take solace in knowing one indisputable fact: I am not alone. The words play over and over in my head, and I can't help but smile. I have waded in a sea of misery and doubt and fear with a dark entity as my only companion for more than ten years, but now I have a lifeline. A connection I thought I would never find again. For the first time in forever, I have hope.

Chapter 6

Shelly called them spectrals. It's good to know they aren't actually spirits. That's one question answered, a million more to go. How many different types of spectrals are there? Where do they come from? Why aren't they in school science books? Shelly said, *We're a dying breed.* Was she talking about others who can see spectrals? Was she being literal or figurative about us dying off? Are we an endangered species being hunted? Am I an alien?

I stare out the window to distract myself. The sun sets behind the Payette National Forest treeline, casting the big sky in twilight blues and purples. Removed from any form of civilized society, this place has no light pollution to dull the encroaching night. With each passing second, the night fills the sky and descends into the forest.

Looking out the window was a bad idea.

Where are we going anyway? I wasn't expecting the Four Seasons, but we're getting beyond the boonies at this point. We haven't driven past a car, a light, or even a road sign in forever. At least the road is paved.

Jeremy hits a deep pothole, banging my head against the window.

"Will there be other kids out here too?" I ask, rubbing the goose egg forming.

Steve nods. "Some have been out here a while. Could probably host their own survival show with all the cool stuff they've learned. Trust me, at no point are you going to be alone."

That's what I'm afraid of. "What if someone gets hurt or a bear attacks or something?"

Steve waves off the question. "There'll be two highly trained wilderness therapists out there with you: Marcus and Shawn. They know these woods like the back of their hands. You're safe and sound with them, but just in case something does happen, they have satellite phones to call for help. But they haven't had to make a call like that for a few years." Steve turns and gives me his best Santa-with-a-plateful-of-cookies smile. "You got nothing to worry about."

"We're here!" Jeremy pulls off the somewhat-paved highway and onto a thin dirt road.

Branches scrape against the side of the van as we make our way along the overgrown path. Ahead, the dirt opens into a small campground with a wooden arch and a busted sign hanging from one rusted chain.

I have to tilt my head to the side to read it: PONDEROSA CAMPGROUND.

The headlights illuminate a small wooden bench at the end of the dirt clearing. Leaning against it is a woman half my size and no more than a hundred pounds, with her arms crossed and military cap pulled low over her eyes. Even from this distance, the scowl below the brim makes me sit up straight. I'm guessing by Jeremy's and Steve's reactions that this is the infamous Shawn.

"She's really very sweet once you get to know her," Jeremy tries but fails to soften the intimidating statue waiting for us. I grab my sketchbook and hop out.

Shawn glances at her watch. "Twenty fifteen. You're supposed to be here at twenty hundred. I'd ask why you're late, but that'll just waste more time, and I'd like to reach camp before we lose all the light."

Shawn glares at the two men towering over her, but her unwavering stare makes them seem small. I'm surprised to see she looks like she's still in college. Her camouflage hat does its best to hide her short brown-highlighted hair pulled in a tight ponytail and her big brown eyes.

The moment she turns that hard glare on me, it vanishes, replaced with a gentle smile. "You must be Cody. I'm Shawn Navarro. I'll be your therapist during your time with us. It's nice to meet you."

Shawn reaches out her hand, and I shake it without a second thought. It's a firm grip, probably from years of having to prove herself to bigger people, but it's also warm. The tension in my shoulders eases a little.

She turns back to my two escorts. "Thank you, gentlemen. I can take it from here."

Steve waves goodbye. "Good luck, Cody."

Jeremy is right behind him. "You got this, my man. Stay strong. Remember, this is a fresh start for you. Be the best Cody you can be."

Let's see Jeremy be the best version of himself with a parasitic nightmare breathing down his neck for a decade. But I bottle the frustration. I've heard it all before with every "fresh start." All I need to do is try harder and things will get better. Like it's my fault. If they could see the darkness haunting me, they wouldn't be so quick to judge.

Steve and Jeremy get in the van and take off. The taillights disappear down the dirt road, and the last sound I hear is tires catching pavement.

Shawn sighs. "We're going to have to skip the formalities if we want to reach basecamp before nightfall." She reaches into her large backpack and pulls out a thick folder. One of the tabs is labeled with my name.

"I have to go over a couple of things here with you, okay? You don't have to answer them if you don't want to, but I'm going to ask that you be completely honest with me. I can't help you if I don't know the truth. That's my number one rule: you don't bullshit me and I don't bullshit you. Deal?"

Sounds great. Honesty is what landed me here in the first place. Does she really expect me to just spill my guts right now and tell her all the shit I've seen and magically be okay?

I've been through this before. My file says past trauma and my inability to cope with the loss of my father mixed with mental illness have led me to this point, so now I need to accept the fact that I need help and blah blah blah. Look at where that's all gotten me—thrown away in the one place that'll probably trigger me the most with a tiny drill sergeant and bunch of teenage nutcases. Awesome.

I just nod.

"Good. First, I see you have no history of drug or alcohol abuse. You've never snuck a drink at a party or something?"

"I don't get invited to a lot of parties."

"No history of self-harm or suicidal ideation?"

I roll my eyes. Couldn't she just read my other therapists' notes? "No. I have not nor have I ever attempted to hurt myself. I started showing symptoms of schizophrenia at the age of four that were exacerbated after the tragic passing of my father. My home life is stressful, and I've had to become the caretaker of my twin sisters since my mother is working—"

"Okay, I get it. You've been through this before." Shawn lowers the checklist. "How about this: it says here you see things you call spirits. Do you think they're real?"

I hesitate. I've had therapists ask this in the past, but there's always a tone of judgment. A hint of mocking me in how they ask the question. They've already decided what the "right" answer is and want to see just how far back I am in the crazy train. But there's no accusation in Shawn's voice; instead it sounds like honest curiosity. She stares back, waiting for my answer.

I find a dirt clod on the ground that needs a good kicking.

"What do they look like? Are they people who have died?"

"They're not ghosts," I blurt out before I can stop myself.

"Okay. So what are they?"

"Almost got me there. Feigning interest. So original." I nod toward the dying light. "I thought you said we were going to be late?"

"Fair enough," Shawn folds up the binder and stuffs it away. "We can finish this on the walk. I'm not going to pressure you into telling me anything you're not ready to. This is a judgment-free place. I'm only here to help you."

She leads me to the bench where a backpack and a ton of gear are laid out. I recognize most of it: canteen, flashlight, a pile of extra clothes, a sleeping bag, tent, some sort of mosquito netting, a small zipped black baggie, and a shovel.

"This is your gear from here on out. You and you alone are responsible for it. You lose it, sucks for you. You break it, better fix it. Tear it, get good with a needle and thread." She reaches over and opens the baggie. "In here you'll find a flint and steel for fire starting, a compass, toothbrush and paste, and a personal locator beacon. Don't be the idiot who loses their personal locator beacon. I recommend you don't even touch it."

"What about, like, ropes and knives and stuff?"

Shawn shakes her head. "Only therapists carry anything that can be used for self-harm. On top of everything you see here, I also have the first-aid kit, multipurpose knife, emergency glow sticks, SAT phone, map, hooks and line for fishing, MREs, bear spray, and a flare gun. Needless to say, if you touch my bag, you're on the next trek outta here.

"As for clothes, you'll wear New Beginnings attire. With winter coming, I recommend layering up, especially at night. If you've never done laundry, learn quick. You'll be in charge of the washing, cleaning, drying, and overall maintenance of your apparel." She hands me the pile of folded clothes.

I raise an eyebrow. "You want me to change? Here? In front of you?"

"You got it. Down to your underwear. Got to make sure you're not smuggling anything into the program. Kids are creative with where they stash things, so we eliminate the risk and give you everything you need. Hurry up. We're losing daylight."

I turn my back to her and change. The tan cargo pants are a little baggy but hold up on their own. At least the bright-orange shirt with the artsy New Beginnings logo of a sun rising over a treeline fits well. The wool socks and boots are a little snug, but I guess they should be if we're going to be hiking all the time.

As I'm tying up my boots, Shawn picks up my sketchbook. "Don't touch that."

She doesn't open it, but she doesn't put it down either. "Sorry, but I have to. I get it—this is yours. Probably means a lot to you since it's your one personal item, but I have to make sure nothing's in here that can hurt you or others. You understand, right?"

"Nothing's in there. Just drawings."

"I want to take you at your word, but for safety purposes—"

"Trust is a one-way thing then, huh? You want it but won't give it." I focus on the laces, hoping the guilt trip is enough to make her put it down.

"Trust is a road we build together, one brick at a time. Right now I have to make sure you're up for the job." With that, Shawn shuffles through each and every page of my book. I imagine she's looking for one thing in particular, but there's no images of Mr. Shadow. Nothing disturbing or demented or any ramblings of a crazy kid haunted by imaginary monsters. I will *never* put Mr. Shadow in there. I get enough of his all-consuming, suffocating presence every day. My sketches help remind me there's more than him out there. The book is half filled with light spectrals I came across recently; it's my way of remembering the beauty and wonder my dad saw. My way of fighting back Mr. Shadow's darkness and holding on to whatever light I can. The last sketch is of Shelly's friend Luna, which I did after we got back in the van.

When I'm done changing, Shawn stands there with my closed sketchbook. "You're incredibly talented. If this is the world you see…" She smiles as I take it back. "Come on. It's time to go."

Shawn helps me pack the rest of the gear and lug it onto my back. It's like carrying Haylee and Kaylee at the same time. How the hell am I going to carry this thing around for the next couple of months?

"So, uh, how far is basecamp?"

"Not too far," Shawn says as she hoists her own backpack like it's stuffed with feathers. "About six and a half kilometers."

"And for those of us born in America?"

"A little over four miles." With a wicked smile, she takes off into the woods. I have to jog to catch up, already feeling the strain on my legs and lungs.

I'm going to die out here.

Chapter 7

I…hate…my…life…

Even my thoughts are out of breath. I have no idea how long we've been going at this. Hours ago I learned to stop asking how much farther. After the third time the distance didn't change, I wanted to lie down and die. I don't even have enough energy to be terrified of Mr. Shadow looming somewhere in the shadows. But Shawn's motivation has kept me going. It's basically this: you get to eat and sleep when you get there, but until then, get your rear in gear.

That and my grumbling stomach keep me moving.

It doesn't help that she doesn't have a bead of sweat on her. I think she gets some kind of sick enjoyment out of watching me suffer. And the whole time she's been talking like we're standing still. It doesn't matter if we were hiking through a ravine, scaling boulders, or cutting through the underbrush, it's like she's taking an easy stroll on the beach.

I've blanked out most of what she said. I haven't done it on purpose; it was more because the blood needed to run my brain was being diverted to the muscles that were about to fail if I tripped over one more tree root.

The gist of it all is this: don't screw up. It's the same speech I've heard from Mom every time we move combined with the lecture I get every time I'm grounded. But the one thing that stuck with me was the acronym Shawn used: A GHOST. It stands for:

Always partner up. Can't even go to the bathroom alone.

Group therapy. Morning and evening with a sprinkling of individuals throughout.

Hygiene. Bathe/shower at every water source. Girls first, then boys.

Ownership. I'm responsible for my stuff and my progress.

Sleep. Sun down, head down. Sun up, wake up.

Team. Help each other get better, so no relationships or harmful comments/acts.

I'm not a fan of the acronym, but at least it's hard to forget.

The only saving grace for this grueling hike is the spectrals. It's been so long since I stepped foot into the forest, I'd forgotten how alive it can be. As the sun disappears, more and more spectrals come out. Light and dark critters of all shapes and sizes fly on translucent wings, swing on their many tails, or dart in and out of the undergrowth. And the sound—the woods are alive with an orchestra of light and music. The hair on my arms stands on end with the wonderful energy coursing around me.

In the distance, a new sound breaks through: laughter coming from a glow dancing behind some bushes. The light of a fire. We've reached camp! Finally I can take this load off.

Shawn stops and turns to me. "We'll walk in and I'll introduce you, okay? This is a good group, so you have nothing to worry about. Ready?"

I try my best to quell my growing nerves. I take a second to collect myself, straighten my sweat-drenched shirt, and take a deep breath. Shawn gives me a reassuring squeeze on the shoulder and we head into camp.

Six bright orange tents create a semicircle around a campfire in the middle of the clearing. String runs from tent to tent with clothes hanging to dry. Around the fire, four people are either sitting on a rock or lying on their backpack.

The smell of barbecue hits my nose and my stomach roars with hunger pains. A man in his thirties with long dreadlocks, a ragged beard, hemp hoodie, and beaded necklace rotates two slabs of meat on a skewer over the fire with a tea kettle on the verge of boiling.

He sees us walk in. "Well, hello there, my compatriots. Welcome to our humble abode."

The others around the fire turn to stare at me.

I realize during the entire hike I came up with nothing to say. "Uh, hey?" I try my best to smile, but it comes across more as a grimace, especially after the hours of hiking. I give a half-hearted wave and am already disappointed with myself. Awesome first impression. Way to start it off strong, Cody.

A synchronized cheer from a boy and girl sitting next to each other welcomes me.

"I knew it!" Even in the light of the fire, the girl's asymmetrical lime-green hair with dark roots stands out. She's on the heavier side, but her wrinkled New Beginnings shirt hides it well. An interesting interwoven pendant with a clear crystal in the center hangs from her neck. "Never doubt the goddess."

The stylish boy next to her finishes an immaculate braid on the short side of her hair. Poised with combed-back black hair, steamed and pressed clothes, and a clean-shaven chiseled face, he looks like he's spent the day at a spa.

Opposite the fire from them, another boy lets out a low groan.

"You good, Deacon?" Shawn asks him.

Deacon smirks. "Was hoping for a hot chick. Gets lonely out here."

Great, one of *those* guys. Every school and psych ward has a Deacon: a good-looking guy rocking a fitted shirt to show off the muscles, wavy hair that always seems to be perfectly kept, and a serious attitude problem.

Shawn glares at him. "Come on, dude. We've been through this."

"What? You want us to be honest, right? Oh, well, guess it'll be nice to get some more testosterone out here. Wait, you're not a fairy too, are you?"

"That's enough." Shawn's sudden, aggressive tone cuts Deacon off.

Deacon rolls his eyes and leans back on his bag. "Whatever."

Shawn turns to the others. "This is Cody, the new intake. Since we're a little late, we'll do the welcome session while we eat. Marcus, how are those rabbits coming along?"

I get a good look at what Marcus is turning over the fire. Two fileted rabbits sizzle. As the smoke wafts up, my stomach growls again.

"Just about there. Pull up a seat, Cody." He slides over on his log. Shawn makes a point to sit on the ground next to Deacon.

"Thanks." I drop my gear and join them. I warm my hands over the fire, thankful for the heat, but can't take my eyes off the roasting rabbits.

"Wondering where they came from?" the stylish boy asks. "Caught them this morning."

"That's… great." My brain wants to be grossed out, but my baser instincts are drooling.

Green-haired girl pulls a bag of roots and berries out of her gear. "If you'd rather not eat something with a face, the Mother always provides." She offers me the bag.

I wave it off. "I'm good."

She shrugs and pops a few berries into her mouth.

"Let's get this welcome group started," Shawn cuts in. She nods to the stylish boy. "Tyler, how about you explain to Cody how they go?"

Tyler clears his throat before starting his practiced explanation. "Welcome groups are designed to introduce you to your fellow—"

"Prisoners," Deacon interjects.

Tyler shoots him a quick glare before continuing. "*Clients* in a safe, comfortable environment. We go around the circle and introduce ourselves, mention what brought us to New Beginnings, and talk about where we are in our treatment."

"Plus, you can discuss anything else you'd like to share, like hobbies, zodiac sign, stuff like that," the green-haired girl adds through a mouthful of berries.

"Then we ask you questions. If you find our lines of inquiry too personal or uncomfortable, you can say, 'pass,' and we won't press for an answer," Tyler finishes.

"We *will* call you a bitch, though."

"Deacon, one more and you'll get another week added," Shawn threatens.

My palms turn to a river of sweat. I'm about to get grilled by a bunch of rehab kids who've been stuck in the woods for God knows how long. This is *not* going to go well.

Marcus steps forward with an armful of dented tin cups. "Dinner is served. A specialty of mine, if I do say so myself. May I present ragoût de lapin. Bon appétit."

Thankful for the distraction, I take a tin cup and see the pulled pieces of what used to be rabbit floating on the surface. Maybe not the distraction I was hoping for. Trying not to think of what the meat used to be, I take a tentative sip.

The warmth hits my empty belly like ink in water and spreads to every part of me. I take another greedy slurp. Before I can catch myself, more than half of my dinner disappears down my throat. I take my first breath in an attempt to savor the rest.

Marcus sits next to me and puts his dreads back into a makeshift ponytail. "Guess I'll start this little shindig off. Name's Marcus Terra. Originally from Albuquerque, New Mexico. I've been a therapist here for—oh, man—going on five years now. Went to a wilderness program when I was your age. I was into a bit of everything, but my main vise was chasing the dragon. Got in the program, found a new natural perspective on things, and now I'm trying to pay it forward."

He glances to his left, where Deacon sits back with his cup of stew. "Deacon Miller. I'm seventeen, a senior from Palos Verdes, California. Four-year lacrosse letterman. Middie. Been here a month for alcoholism, depression, and anger issues. Currently working on controlling my outbursts and thinking before I speak. Working wonders so far."

"Hi, I'm Meadow Sanchez." The green-haired girl beams. "Oh, let me see. I'm sixteen, newly practicing wiccan from Boulder, Colorado, and I'm an Aquarius, so that pretty much tells you all you need to know right there. I'm here for depression, self-harm, suicidal ideation, and a couple of attempts. I got here a few weeks ago and am *loving* it. Really helps me get in touch with the Mother. And I'm working on…what was that term, Marcus?"

"Masking."

"That's it. I'm working on taking off my mask and showing how I really feel."

"And you're doing great at it," Tyler says, and gives her a one-armed hug. "Guess it's my turn. My name's Tyler Pung and I'm fifteen from Boston, Mass. I'm half Italian and half Korean. I run track for my school, class president, and help organize a nonprofit scholarship program for students who can't afford proper food or clothing. I should be leaving in a few weeks if my parents allow it, and I'm working on my depression, anxiety, OCD, eating disorder, and self-acceptance."

Deacon chuckles. "That it? Where's that self-acceptance you were just talking about?"

Tyler chews on the inside of his cheek before answering. "And... I'm g-g-gay."

I sit in silence, listening to each of their little introductions. How were they being so candid? No one in their right mind would admit to half the stuff I just heard, yet here they all are, talking about alcoholism, suicide, and their sexual identity like it's the weather. I've been in a few groups before, but this one is way more relaxed. Open.

"And you know me," Shawn adds with a warm smile. "I'm originally from the Philippines but moved to the states when I was nine. Lost my way with a bad crowd but found a new home in the Air Force. After an honorable discharge, had a hard time acclimating to civilian life. PTSD, alcoholism, anger issues, the works. I got the help I needed, then found this program, and it's been smooth sailing since."

"Okay, your turn," Meadow chirps up. She leans in, ready for my story, but the count is off. Shawn, Marcus, Meadow, Tyler, and Deacon make five people—there are six tents.

"Still got one more, Meadow," Shawn says, confirming my thoughts. "Kekoa, can you please join the group?"

I follow her gaze and see someone sitting on the outskirts of the firelight, arms hugging knees to chest. All I can see under the hoodie is olive skin and a pair of headphone wires hanging out that plug into something in her pouch.

Deacon takes an exasperated breath. "Not this shit again. Can't we just do the intro for her? This is Kekoa Make Any—"

"It's pronounced Makanani," Tyler grumbles.

"Whatever. She's from Hawaii and—"

"You're not helping," Tyler barks back.

"And here comes the white knight in his shining armor. Or would you prefer pink?"

"Deacon, you and me, one on one, now." Shawn stands and waits for Deacon to join her.

"This is bullshit. Why does she get special treatment?" Deacon snaps back. He jumps to his feet but doesn't follow Shawn. Instead he takes a step toward Kekoa and reaches for her headphones. "Earth to Kekoa. How about you check in and—"

Kekoa's hands are a blur. Just as Deacon wraps his fingers around her headphones, she grabs him by the wrist and twists his arm, bringing the much larger kid to his knees. She follows it up with a quick jerk and slams Deacon to the ground, holding his arm behind his back.

"Let go, you crazy-ass bitch." Deacon squirms but can't escape the hold.

Kekoa takes her headphones back. "Touch me again and I'll break it off." She lets his arm go and storms off to her tent.

"I got her," Shawn says as she hurries after Kekoa.

Deacon sits up, dusts himself off, and rubs his sore shoulder. Marcus just shakes his head, "Not cool, dude. Not cool."

"What? It's not like she's listening to anything. You just let her get away with ignoring everyone here."

"You can't rush treatment. Regression to the mean. Kekoa will get there, in her time."

"She's been out here, what, at least twice as long as Tyler? She hasn't even told us why she's here in the first place. How long's it going to take?"

"As long as she needs," Marcus says with a tone of finality. "Now back to where we were. Cody, how about you tell us a little bit about yourself?"

I try to gather my thoughts after that little show. "Yeah, sure. So I'm Cody. I'm seventeen. I've kinda moved around a lot, but right now I live in Cedar Hills, California. I'm here for…" I hesitate. I can't just spit out that I'm diagnosed with schizophrenia. I'll be ostracized on the first night. "I'm here for anxiety, anger, depression, and substance abuse." I'd spent enough time in psych wards to know explainable diagnoses.

As Marcus raises an eyebrow, I remember my file in Shawn's backpack. Of course he must have read through it before my arrival. No way they would take on clients without knowing everything about them.

I wait for Marcus to out me, but he just shrugs. "So who has the first question?"

Tyler raises his hand as if he were in school, but Meadow beats him to the punch. "If you were a popsicle, what flavor would you be, how long would it take for you to melt, and what would the joke be on the stick?"

Seriously? Out of all the questions she could possibly ask, especially with how vague I was, she wants to know what kind of popsicle I would be?

I try and think of the last time I had a popsicle, and then I remember a weekend at the fair where I split one with my sisters. "Orange Creamsicle. I'd be the kind that never melts so I wouldn't get messy. And the joke? Um, oh…I got one. What's a pirate's favorite letter?"

"That's easy. It's the *R*," Tyler says with a satisfied smirk. "Because pirates say 'Arr.'"

I give my best pirate impersonation. "You think it's the *R,* but 'tis the *C*."

It at least gets a laugh from Meadow. "That's the best answer ever!"

"Okay, enough with the weird softball questions," Deacon cuts in. "You said you were here for substance abuse. Drug of choice?"

There's the question I was expecting. Kids in the ward did this too, a screwed-up way of measuring your cool factor. The harder the drug, the more cred you had. It was also easy to smell the bull. Kids would lie but were outed pretty quick and stuck on the bottom of the psych-ward social hierarchy. My best bet was always just to tell the truth, to an extent.

"Seroquel."

Deacon's eyebrows shoot up in surprise. "That shit'll get you screwed up quick. Full-on outta-body experience. Must've gotten it pretty cheap, though."

And there's the test. Amateur. "Mom has a prescription," I lie. "Didn't dabble too much. Mostly sold it for double the price." Best to hide lies in the truth.

This gets a complimentary nod from Deacon, who seems satisfied with the answer.

To break the line of questioning, Marcus leans in. "How are you doing after the pickup?"

Tyler sits up at the question. "Did the night ninjas get you?"

"The what?"

"Not the nicest nickname for our transport team," Marcus answers.

"You mean Steve and Jeremy? Yeah, they came to the house and picked me up. Nice guys, I guess. Got me a burger at Shelly's Diner."

"Oh, please don't do that," Tyler requests. "First thing you'll learn out here is you cannot, under any circumstances, talk about real-world food. Makes things harder on everyone."

Before I can respond, footsteps approach. Shawn with the hooded Kekoa in tow take their seats around the fire, and even though I can't see her eyes, I feel Kekoa staring daggers at Deacon. He lays back, unfazed.

"We do the superpower one yet?" Shawn asks. Marcus shakes his head. "Awesome. That's my favorite. Okay, Cody, if you had a superpower, what would it be and why?"

I mentally run through the list of superheroes I know and their powers. Flying is always a popular choice—or strength, invisibility, or doing stuff with your mind. But I can't choose one, until I realize why. I already have a power and I'd do anything to get rid of it. "I wouldn't want one. I just want to be normal."

As soon as I say my answer, I see Kekoa's head perk up. Her eyes, an intense green, stare back at me with curiosity.

"Worst answer ever," Deacon scoffs.

"Actually it's rather intuitive," Marcus counters. "Color me impressed. I would have guessed shapeshifting. Clients tend to wish they could be someone else."

Shawn stands and stretches. "With that, it's time for bed, ladies and gentlemen. Even though we had a late intake, we're still up at first light. You'll have plenty of time to get to know Cody over the next few weeks. You've got fifteen minutes to pack it in. Tyler, you're partnering with Cody for the night. Help him set up his tent."

Deacon tries to repress a snort. "Oh, he'll help him get his tent up all right."

"Deacon!" Shawn snaps as Tyler turns a new shade of red.

"What? You can't expect me to let a lob like that go. It's your fault really."

With that, the meal is over. As everyone loads their gear into their tents, I pull mine out and stare at it. My fingers won't move, frozen by the reality of where I am. My throat tightens and my heart crashes into the back of my ribs like a runaway Mack truck. The last time I went camping...

"It won't bite," Tyler jokes as he picks up the tent. "Come on. Just follow my lead." I do what I can, but it's mostly Tyler ordering me to hold a rod here or stomp a pin there. It takes a minute, but my tent is up and ready to go.

I thank Tyler and slide into my tent as Shawn walks over. "Marcus or I will be out here for the night shift if you need anything, all right? Get some rest."

I doubt I'll get any. "Yeah, good night." I zip up the tent behind me and get in my bag.

It's not the most comfortable I've been. The ground is hard, there's a chill in the air, and the woods are loud: crickets, owls, even the high-pitched screech of bats, but the spectrals stand out most. Their sound is different, more somber, like the calls of a humpback whale deep below the ocean's surface. I've never felt so small compared to the massive world outside my tent. I'm both in awe and terrified with how exposed I feel out here.

Chapter 8

Deacon walks down a school hallway chatting with a few of his lacrosse buddies. He nods at a small underclassman hiding under his headphones headed in their direction. As they cross paths, Deacon slams the kid into a metal locker, knocking him to the ground.

A woman's distorted voice screams from the other side of a bedroom door: *What's wrong with you? Your father and I did not raise you to be like this! You're just confused. It's a phase...*

Green hair dye, eyeliner, foundation, concealer, and so much more have been pushed to the side on the bathroom sink. Front and center is a razor blade.

My eyes snap open and I struggle to catch my breath. All I want to do is take a bath. I feel dirty invading the others' lives like this—stealing their secrets. I don't want to know any of this, but Mr. Shadow has other plans.

I throw the claustrophobic sleeping bag off and rip the tent's zipper down; I need fresh air. I've had dreams or visions or whatever these are before, but these were way more intense. I wasn't just there—I could almost feel what the others were going through.

A freezing breeze stings my exposed skin. I glance up at the cloudless night framed by the silhouette of evergreen trees. I've never seen so many stars. High above the trees, a dark figure drifts across the sky. I almost ignore it as a passing cloud, until two red dots flash open and peer down at me.

"The first night's always the hardest," Marcus says as he lays another branch in the fire. He pats the ground next to him. "Pop a squat."

I glance back up, but the red-eyed apparition is gone. I grab my jacket and join Marcus by the fire.

"The woods at night have a different vibe than during the day, you know? Like you can totally feel the energy flowing all around."

I choose my words carefully. "You believe in that kind of thing? Energies we can't see?"

"For sure. Think about it. Before we had the technology, no one knew what infrared or ultraviolet were. A campfire was just a fire; it gave heat. Now we know some of the heat radiating from it is actually infrared radiation. Energy we can't see. The wavelength spectrum is huge, yet we can only see a small fraction of it. For all we can see, our world is actually very limited."

"Sounds deep."

He chuckles. "Yeah, sorry about that. I had some pretty heavy conversations when my buddies and I got high. One stuck with me, though, really helped when I decided to get clean. His name was Hashkeh, Hash for short. He was part of the local Navajo tribe. You want to talk about a culture that believes in unseen energies… Anyway, one day we were coming down and I don't remember why, but he just started laughing. The guy was always happy, no matter what, and I asked him, 'Hash, how are you always so happy?' And you know what he said?

"He said we all feed on the energies we surround ourselves with. That inside each of us are two hungry wolves, insatiable, locked in a constant battle. One is good and kind; the other is angry and fearful. The one that wins is the one you feed. So he decided he was going to feed the good wolf and surround himself with positivity."

"And is that what you did to, uh, get clean?"

Marcus smiles and shakes his head. "Not even close. It took me a few more years and an overdose to get me out of my hole. But once I started to climb out, I realized Hash was onto something. We become the energy we put out, good or bad. Some people call it an aura, others call it gut or instinct, but we all have that sixth sense that picks up on others' energies. So now I try to feed my good wolf. How about you, Cody? Which wolf do you feed?"

Before I answer, another breeze rushes through camp. The fire struggles against the chilling blast and the trees dance in the flickering light. Only one shadow holds steady.

Mr. Shadow stands outside the clearing, his black static figure looming tall in the distance. The shimmer of his hat nearly touches the bottom of the branches.

Marcus? Oh, God, Marcus! Mom, he's not breathing! Call 911!

I'm standing next to a young girl with thick, black-framed glasses shaking a younger unconscious Marcus with a needle stuck in his arm. I can smell the bile, feel the burn of the needle, the cold creeping through my body...

"Hey, Cody. You good, buddy?"

I fight the urge to throw up. "Your sister was the one who found you?" I ask, still caught with the split-second image of a young girl and dying brother.

"How...how did you know?" Marcus asks, sitting up a little.

Realizing my slip-up, I try to blow it off. "Lucky guess. Just reading the energies or something, right?" I get up from my seat and head back toward my tent. "Thanks for the talk. I feel better now. I think I'm gonna try and get some sleep."

Before Marcus can respond, I shuffle into my tent and zip it closed behind me.

This is a whole new level for Mr. Shadow. I felt the needle in my arm, felt myself dying. What's happening? How is Mr. Shadow doing this? And more disconcerting...why?

I slide into my sleeping bag and pull it tight to fight away the growing chill. Not from the cold, but from the thoughts racing through my mind.

One scares me the most: Mr. Shadow is getting stronger. And if that's true, we're in trouble. Mr. Shadow is my bad wolf, and if he's feeding on negative energy, I've just taken him to an all-you-can-eat buffet.

Chapter 9

It feels like the moment I fall asleep, an airy whine wakes me up. I poke my head out to see what's dying and have to shield my eyes from the morning sun.

Marcus pulls the harmonica from his lips. "A wonderful first good morning to you, my friend. You like your alarm clock?"

Deacon's voice comes from behind the tents. "Please, for the love of everything holy, shove that thing where the sun don't shine!"

"Everyone's a critic." Marcus shrugs before bringing the harmonica back to his mouth.

In the morning light, the woods have transformed from dark and ominous to warm and welcoming. A gentle breeze rustles the leaves, and the air has an earthy pine smell to it.

The others are busy with their morning routines. Deacon and Tyler are outside the circle of tents, in the middle of a serious workout. Deacon, shirtless with a sheen of sweat, powers through a set of push-ups. Tyler struggles to keep pace.

"Five more, princess. Let's go!" Deacon barks as he leans on Tyler's back.

"You're not helping," Tyler pants.

"You want to get big, you need to push it. Fight through the resistance!"

Tyler collapses on the fourth. "You're p-p-pushing too hard."

"You quit too soon. I told you this wouldn't be easy. So sack up if you got one and finish strong, you pansy!"

Deacon lifts Tyler by the shirt and forces him into a pushup position. With quaking arms, Tyler powers through the last two and collapses.

"Get your ass up!" Deacon grabs a low-hanging branch as Tyler struggles to stand up. "We got pull-ups next."

Don't these guys get enough of a workout with all the hiking? Happy with not joining them, I see Meadow sitting in a small dirt circle talking to herself. A beam of light breaks through the trees and shines on her like a spotlight. As I listen, I realize she's praying.

"Of gracious Goddess, I ask thee to bless this day. To bring joy and light along my way. Guide my heart, my hands, my voice, to honor Thee with every choice. Blessed Be."

She kisses the crystal within her woven pendant necklace and rises to her feet. "I'll see what I can gather for breakfast," she announces before heading off into the woods.

"A!" Tyler yells between pull-ups. "Always partner up."

"Wait until Shawn gets back and I'll go with you," Marcus calls back.

"Hey, Marcus," I say. "Where's Shawn?"

"Morning session with Kekoa. They headed to the stream to catch us some breakfast. Should be back soon. Did Shawn go over the morning routine on the walk in?"

Great, more rules and regulations, and here I thought I'd gotten out of going to prison.

"There's a few things that need to get done every morning before we can head out, so we divide out the responsibilities. There's gathering food for breakfast, packing up the tents and gear, and cleaning the site. Today Tyler and Kekoa are on food duty; you and Deacon are breaking down the tents; and Meadow's got clean-up. Once that's all done, we get going."

Deacon gives me a wet slap on the back. "Let's get this over with, newbie. I wanna hit that stream and wash off before we head out."

Breaking down a tent is a lot easier than getting it up. They just fall over when I touch them. The hard part is packing them tightly enough to fit in the bottom loops of the backpacks. Deacon isn't the best instructor—his way of teaching is more yelling than showing.

By the time we finish, Kekoa and Shawn have returned with three decent-size trout; Marcus and Meadow have collected a bag full of edible vegetation; and Tyler's traps have snared a squirrel.

"A feast fit for kings and queens," Marcus says as he preps the food.

Shawn fishes out a box from her backpack and uses the orange key around her neck to unlock it. "Time for meds."

I forgot about my medication. It's not like I've been taking it, but I didn't think about the others. It makes sense that the counselors would also be in charge of giving us our daily doses.

One by one, everyone lines up and takes their pills. I'm last, right behind Kekoa, who's dressed in her typical sweatpants and long sleeves with her hoodie up and earbuds in. She gives me a quick glance over her shoulder but doesn't say anything.

I try to say hello, but she turns back, leaving me with my mouth half open.

Shawn holds out a clear cup overflowing with pills. "Are you taking them today?" The hoodie shakes side to side. "You have to verify verbally."

"No."

"I'm going to have to notify your dad. You know that, right?"

Kekoa shrugs and walks away.

My turn. Shawn holds out my daily dose of Seroquel. "So you can refuse your meds?"

She nods. "This isn't the psych ward. We're not going to force them down your throat, but if you refuse three times in a row, we have to notify your legal guardian."

"What happens then?"

"Well, it's up to the guardian at that point. We've had clients get removed from the program and checked into the hospital. Other times a psychiatrist is consulted and they prescribe something different. Most of the time, after a day or two, the clients start feeling like crap and realize they need the meds, so they start taking them again. So what's it going to be?"

Shawn offers the medication. Even without turning around, I feel the others watching. Seeing how new intakes handle meds was always an entertaining show in the ward. You could tell how screwed up a kid was by how they acted. Did they swallow or cheek, cause a scene or be docile, accept their situation or deny it all?

"No, thanks."

Shawn puts the meds back in her backpack. "Okay. That's day one. Two more and we have to make that call. Got it?"

"Got it." I have zero intention of ever taking them, so that gives me two more days to figure out what I'm going to do. If they call my mom, she'll have me arrested or committed. I could sell them again, but if anyone here mixed meds it could be bad. My best bet is to cheek them, but what do I do with them after? Can't really toss bright-yellow pills in a forest of green. Maybe I could bury them if I get enough alone time... I'm going to have to get creative with this.

Shawn and I rejoin the others in the broken-down camp. Marcus puts the final pieces of fish on each plate and hands them out. "Breakfast is served."

Maybe because I'm not starving like I was last night or maybe it's because I can actually see the food in the morning light, but getting a serving of roots, fish, and the thin bones of a squirrel on a tin plate makes my stomach curl. Haylee and Kaylee have prepared more appetizing breakfasts, and they use rainbow sprinkles on everything.

The others don't hesitate. Meadow chows down on her veggies and laughs with Tyler; Deacon inhales the meats while avoiding the greens; even Kekoa has started on the second half of her plate.

When in Rome…

I take a safe bite of the trout and am surprised yet again. Whatever Marcus does with the limited supplies he has is close to magic. It tastes like it came from Tomasso's, a restaurant we only go to on birthdays. I try the plants and even brave the squirrel. Although the meat is a little tough, it still goes down easily.

Before long, all our plates are cleaned and we're ready for morning group.

I dread this part the most: a bunch of kids with chips on their shoulders sitting in a circle being asked to reveal their secrets. The last time I did this, the orderlies had to be called in to break up a fight.

But at the same time, if I want to get out of here, I have to play the game. I can't sit back and go silent; that just aggravates the therapists and wastes everyone's time. So, to get back home, the best course of action is the one I want to take the least: tell the truth…mostly.

Marcus rubs his hands together. "Today's focus topic is one of our favorites; family."

This word is met with a chorus of groans. Even under the hoodie, I see Kekoa roll her eyes and retreat farther into the shadows.

"They're part of your lives, whether you like it or not," Marcus smirks. "They've also had a massive impact on all the things that have led you to this moment, both good and bad. I know it's tough, but we could really help each other with this."

"I want to focus on how to have a voice back home," Shawn continues. "Sometimes we scream at our family or completely shut down. How many times have you been arguing about grades, the friends you hang out with, the responsibilities around the house—"

"The handle you stole from your dad's sock drawer," Deacon jokes.

"Or that, but you don't know how to say your piece without making things worse? It's because there's a breakdown in communication. One or both sides don't feel like they're being heard. That adds fuel to the fire. So what do we do when we don't feel like we're being heard?"

"I shut down," Tyler starts. "My parents are very particular about my grades, my clothes, my presentation, even how I talk to them. For Koreans, one must respect their elders. I can't talk back or even voice my opinion. My mom's rule is law and I must obey, no matter how I feel."

Marcus rests his chin in his hands. "So you sit there and take it. You internalize your voice and let your mom say whatever she wants. What happens when you try to speak up?"

"It gets worse. But I feel I've gotten better with this and I know my voice matters."

Now there's a treatment line if I've ever heard one. Guess I'm not the only one playing the game to get out of here as fast as possible.

"Maybe either the words you use or the way you say them triggers something in your mom," chimes in Meadow. "I know when my parents start yelling at me, if I just agree with them, they stop a lot sooner and leave me alone."

"Yeah, that's healthy," Deacon scoffs. "You do realize your parents are human, right? They can be wrong. A lot."

Shawn nods. "That's a good point. Parents might not always be right, but they might also be working with limited information. Deacon, when your dad yells at you, do you ever think if he just knew what you were thinking, he'd understand and you wouldn't have to get into a fight?"

Deacon shakes his head. "I think he needs to stop being a drunk dumbass. He doesn't give a damn—he just needs a punching bag and I'd rather it be me than Jason."

"Who's Jason?" I ask.

"Just the cutest little brother ever." Meadow beams. "Oh! Show him your picture!"

Deacon's jaw clenches and he cracks his neck. I've seen that before: universal bully warnings. They're pissed and someone's about to feel it.

But Shawn is quick to change the focus. "Another time. How about you, Cody? You and your mom get along?"

I shrug, uncomfortable now that the attention is on me. "Sure. We're fine most of the time."

Shawn doesn't let me off the hook. "What happens the rest of the time?"

"There's more yelling than anything else, but she's stressed and she's not about to yell at my little twin sisters, so I'm her anger displacement." I realize my slip-up too late.

"Sounds like someone's been to treatment before," Deacon says with a smile.

"We've had a couple of bad ones," I confess. "She called a 5150 on me."

"That's a seventy-two-hour hold," Tyler chimes in. "A danger to yourself or others."

"Let me guess—you were hopped up on that Susie-Q and started seeing crazy shit," Deacon adds.

If he considers a demonic shadow haunting me for more than a decade "crazy shit," then yeah. "Something like that."

Marcus leans in. "Cody, I'm going to push you a little here, okay? When you see things, do you tell your mom?"

I was right: he did read my file. Great, it's going to be impossible to keep my secret now. I'm not exactly mentally ready to discuss this out loud. I just shake my head.

Marcus continues. "She may be a supermom, but she can't read your mind. How is she supposed to help you if you won't let her in?"

"Maybe she can't handle the truth," Kekoa answers.

I turn to her, sitting on the ground just outside the circle. We make eye contact. Her face would make a professional poker player second-guess himself, but her emerald eyes stare back at me with intensity.

"What do you mean?" Shawn asks.

Kekoa stares at me a second longer. Then, with a shrug, she turns to Shawn. "We don't just decide one day not to trust our parents. It's something we're taught. We reach out but get left behind. Maybe Cody told the truth and his mom didn't want to hear it or didn't believe it too many times, so he stopped telling her. Maybe he stopped letting her in to protect himself."

The other clients' jaws are on the ground. It seems Kekoa's insight has caught everyone off guard. For me, it's her accuracy that's so shocking. She's spot-on. No one has ever come close to putting into words why I don't trust my mom.

"I guess being out here forever and a day really paid off," Deacon jabs, breaking the awkward silence. "Just get a license, and you could be one of the therapists instead."

Marcus nods in agreement. "We'd be honored to have you." He gets up and grabs his gear. "That'll do it for this morning, ladies and gentlemen. Time to head off on another great adventure. During the hike, your assignment is to grab a partner and continue our awesome discussion. Find out about each other's families, where they come from, what it's like at home. And really listen." He turns to Meadow and Tyler. "And before you ask, no, you two cannot be partners."

As we pack up, Tyler rushes over to me. "How'd you get Kekoa to talk?"

"I didn't do anything."

"Since I've been here, I can count on one hand the number of times we've actually exchanged words.

Then you show up, and this is the first morning that she's spoken in complete sentences. You're the only variable."

All I can do is shrug my shoulders. I honestly have no idea what I did.

Tyler relents. "Should be interesting. Anyway, you mind if we partner up? Deacon's a jerk and Kekoa kinda scares me."

"I was actually thinking of…" I scan for Kekoa. I want to ask her a few questions, but she's walking with Shawn. "You know what? Sure."

A few minutes later and we're off, following Marcus deeper into the woods. All evidence of our presence in the small clearing is gone except for a few footprints.

Tyler and I talk the entire walk. He's actually a nice kid. We discuss our moms and their inabilities to step outside their comfort zones and listen to us, but it eventually evolves into friends, school, and life in general. I have a hard time finding anything wrong with him. Maybe the only reason he's here *is* because his mom doesn't accept the fact that he's gay.

I'm also having a hard time finding anything wrong with New Beginnings. It's different from the psych wards. Out here, the group seems looser, freer, and willing to be themselves and accepting of others. The air is fresh; the woods are lush; and I feel the weight on my shoulders chip away with every step. If only the backpack would lighten too.

Watching vibrant spectrals scurry up trees and dart through the underbrush doesn't hurt either. They go about their day, ignoring us, save one. When we cross a small creek, there's a dark mountain lion with six legs and thorny bramble antlers watching us with a passive curiosity. Blissfully ignorant of the spectral, the others go on their merry way.

I'm surprised to feel no blast of cold from it like I do when Mr. Shadow's around. No sense of danger at all. Just awe at its strength and beauty.

And as soon as we cross the water, the dark spectral saunters away into the woods.

Who knows? Maybe this whole wilderness thing won't be so bad after all.

Chapter 10

Wake up, break down, gather food, meds, morning process, hike, first activity, lunch, hike, second activity, set up, gather food, evening process, bed.

Wake up, break down, gather food, meds, morning process, hike, first activity, lunch, hike, second activity, set up, gather food, evening process, bed.

Day after day, the regimen is drilled so deeply into my head I feel like my DNA has changed. I've become a mad scientist's wilderness robot. To break the monotony of the routine, I sketch every spectral I see. By the time the first two weeks go by, I'm near the end of my sketchbook.

There were a few times when someone would break the pattern. Deacon tried to throw a coup one morning and refused to get out of his tent. He broke when Marcus cooked up some rabbit for breakfast.

Another time, Meadow slipped down a hill and got stuck in a ravine. Shawn repelled down like Spider-Man and was able to hoist her out.

The most recent event occurred when a button on Tyler's pants went missing and he refused to leave camp until it was found. After an hour of searching, Deacon fessed up that he had ripped it off in the night and pocketed the button. His reason? "If he thinks he's good to go home, he needs to be okay with his world not being perfect. One little button isn't a big deal. Obviously he's not ready." Tyler didn't talk to Deacon for two days.

I'm not a fan of morning meds, though. To be more precise, I don't like lying to Shawn and Marcus. After refusing to take them two days in a row, I knew on the third they were going to contact my mom. So I did the only thing I could think of: I cheeked them. Years of practice made it easy to get it by even Marcus's trained eye.

Then I pocketed them. No use wasting the pills. Someone's always going to be willing to pay—all I have to do is hide them until I get discharged.

As weird as it sounds, there is a sort of peace in the simplicity of it all. I don't have to worry about doing homework, picking up Haylee and Kaylee, or if Mom and I will fight about something. I just have to take care of me.

I've even caught myself laughing a few times. It's hard to see everyone as intakes after being around them every second of every day. We're a ragtag group of misfits cast away from society because we don't fit its cookie cutter mold. Our outsiderness bonds us.

Tyler is an energetic encyclopedia of wilderness knowledge but still battles his OCD tendencies and eating disorder. I've seen him switch plates with Deacon to make it look like he's eaten all his food while Deacon gets double servings.

Meadow is a ball of sunshine, bringing light to even the darkest moments in a session. We call it her silver-lining mask, but she's still having a hard time taking it off and showing us what's really going on underneath.

I can always rely on Deacon for a sarcastic comment or snappy retort, but the withdrawals still hit him sometimes and he can get flat-out mean.

The only one I don't have a decent grip on is Kekoa. After she defended me, she retreated back into her hoodie and headphones. I catch her observing me with those intense green eyes when she thinks I'm not paying attention. As soon as I turn to her, she turns away. She still hasn't shared during group either. The others have a bet on why she's at New Beginnings. Winner gets their laundry done for a week. Meadow thinks she's dealing with severe depression. Tyler's going with speed addiction since it's the most common drug in Hawaii. Deacon is convinced she's on the run for murder.

I'm staying out of it. I know that look; it's the same one I've been staring at in the mirror for the last ten years. Something happened. But like Marcus said, she'll tell us in her own time. For now I'm happy just exchanging a few words a day with her.

Then there's Mr. Shadow. He's the last part of the routine. He visits every night as I lay in my sleeping bag and whispers to me. He tells me everyone's secrets, things they haven't even shared during group. I see the horrible traumas they've been through. I've smelled the breath of Deacon's abusive alcoholic father, felt the cut of Meadow's razor, and tasted the bile as Tyler vomits his dinner. I've even heard the cries of wounded men and women as bullets whizz by Shawn's ear and watched Marcus's veins turn black around the needle.

The only person Mr. Shadow hasn't violated is Kekoa. She's an absolute mystery. I don't know why, and to be honest, I don't want to know. I'm enjoying the quiet. I feel at peace around her, even if she doesn't acknowledge my existence. There are no voices, no terrible images; it's just the two of us. When I'm around her, I feel normal.

This morning's routine has been no different. Marcus serenaded us with his ever-stagnate harmonica skills. Tyler checked the overnight traps, but for the third day in a row he came back with nothing. Luckily enough, Meadow was able to gather some berries and roots. That plus two of Shawn's food rations covered us for breakfast.

Kekoa and I broke down the tents. By this point I've become a master, but I don't mind the help. Deacon worked out since there were no plates to clean. Shawn led a morning group about taking ownership of our actions and not letting situations outside our control dictate how we feel. So exciting.

With morning group done, Marcus loads up his gear and rubs his hands together. "I've got good news. You know what today is?"

Meadow perks up and pulls on Tyler's arm. "Ooh, ooh, how long's it been?"

Tyler does some calculations in his head before a huge smile crosses his face. "It's been twenty-eight days!"

"You're joking," Deacon asks, restraining his excitement as best he can. "Pool drop?"

Marcus nods. A unanimous cheer erupts from the three teens. The faintest of smiles shines from under Kekoa's hoodie. I, on the other hand, am confused.

"What's pool drop?" I ask. "Are we going into town or something?"

"We receive a resupply drop once a month at a natural pool a couple of miles from here," Marcus answers. "Steve and Jeremy load up on all the necessary equipment we need: food rations, meds, and toiletries, plus anything extra we radio in for."

"Why don't they just bring it to us?"

Shawn shakes her head. "We used to, but the previous transport team was a little too trusting and thought they were helping the kids by bringing letters. They never checked the envelopes. The kids got their hands on things they shouldn't have. It's just a safety precaution."

"You're going to love the pool." Meadow beams. "There's a picturesque waterfall surrounded by the most vibrant flowers you've ever seen. The water's freezing, but you get used to it. And last time I found a bird's nest with eggs. I wonder if they've hatched?! Oh, and with the supply drop, that means no more leaves to—"

"What Meadow's trying to say is we get to have some fun," Tyler cuts in.

"We've still got a couple of hours," Shawn says. "So on the way, we're going to partner up and discuss times when you should've taken ownership over your choices and where they led you. Also talk about the times when you let others' actions control how you thought and felt."

Shawn turns to Meadow before she can rush to Tyler's side. "We've got a one-on-one today, so Tyler's with Deacon and Cody's with Kekoa. Any questions?"

"Can I just stab my ears now?" Deacon groans. "As much as I would love to listen to three hours about his homophobic parents and OCD issues—"

"Maybe you can bestow some of your special candid honesty on him and help Tyler see how remarkable he already is," Marcus tries.

Deacon pretends to gag. Tyler just sulks away.

From previous walks with Kekoa, I know the next few hours will be filled with nothing but the sounds of the woods. A constant orchestra of bugs, birds, small animals, and the melodic hum of the spectrals. Peaceful.

What's strange is, in the last couple of days, the music seems to have been turned down. Fewer birds, chipmunks, critters, even spectrals. It all started around the same time Tyler stopped catching breakfast in the mornings.

But as we walk, a melodic tune catches my ear, one I haven't heard before. It's soft and soothing. I pull my sketchbook, ready to sketch the new spectral, but I don't see it. It takes me a second to realize the faint music is coming from under the dark hoodie next to me. Kekoa is humming to herself.

I hold my breath, afraid that if she realizes I've noticed, she'll stop. I try to act normal, but suddenly my feet don't know how to walk. I've never heard such a dulcet voice before. Even the spectrals nearby stop and listen, just as entranced as I am.

A sparrow light spectral with four wings and tiny cat's paws flutters down from a branch and floats above Kekoa's head. It drifts back and forth with the melody, dancing on the breeze.

This is perfect.

I open my sketchbook and get to work. I start with the spectral just in case it flies away. After weeks of drawing these guys, I get it on the page pretty quick. Then I move on to Kekoa and her hoodie. I haven't drawn anyone from the group yet, so I try to focus on getting the details right. I sketch the drawstrings, the shadows as they fall on her button nose, the dimples that form at the corner of her soft lips as she sings…

I glance up for the final touches and freeze. Kekoa stares at me. My throat dries up as I stammer out an apology. "I'm so… I didn't mean to. I just thought—"

"What's that?" Kekoa points to the spectral floating above her head in my sketch.

I try to think of an excuse. "It's…uh…your voice?" What the hell does that even mean?!

She raises an eyebrow. For a second, I get the feeling she knows I'm lying. I don't know how, but there's something in those eyes that knows more. "My voice?"

"Yeah. I mean, I was listening, and—I don't know—that's what it sounds like to me." I try to bury my sketchbook in my bag like I want to bury myself in the ground.

"It's...nice."

I stop. Was that a compliment? I spot a faint smile and if I didn't know better, I'd swear she was blushing under that hoodie.

"Where'd you learn to draw like that?"

"My dad was an art teacher. He used to come home with paint or chalk or charcoal all over him. My mom would get mad 'cause the paint would mess up the laundry, but he'd just laugh. He bought me my first sketchbook. Been doodling in them ever since."

"He must be proud."

"I hope so. He, uh, died."

"I'm sorry."

If I could shove my foot any farther into my mouth, I'd be chewing on my knee. Here I am, finally talking to the one person in the world I can be normal around, and in five seconds I've made it awkward as hell.

"How about you? What's your family like?"

Kekoa doesn't respond right away, and for a moment I'm afraid I've ruined any chance of talking to this girl, but then she sighs. "Normal until I was ten. Then one day Mom up and left for the mainland. Dad blamed me cause she and I butted heads a lot. She was always trying to tell me what to do, and I kinda have an issue with authority. So she was gone and he checked out too. He was never really there for me to begin with, so it wasn't anything new. He wanted a son. That's why he named me Kekoa."

And I thought my family was complicated. "What does Kekoa mean?"

"It's a boy's name. Means 'warrior.'"

"After watching you put Deacon on the ground my first night, the name kinda suits you."

For the first time since I've met Kekoa, she smiles. A teeth-showing, eye-squinting, genuinely happy smile. She tries to shrug off the compliment, unsure of how to handle her face. "I've gotten in a scrape or two back home with some of the local boys."

"Yeah, sure. One or two. More like you're a secret black belt."

And the smile widens. As we walk and talk, all I want to do is make sure that smile never leaves her face. She's a different person; the rain cloud over her is gone, and the sunlight is finally breaking through. Kekoa hides it well, under her long sweats and hoodie, but she's actually really pretty.

I snap back to reality and realize I'm staring. She glares back, but there's a playfulness in it. I'm only slightly terrified for my safety. I try to salvage some dignity. "So, I have to know, what's with the headphones? They aren't plugged into anything, so why wear them?"

Kekoa reaches up and touches the headphones in her ears as if she forgot they were there. Then, with a slight hesitation, she takes them out and pockets them. "No one bothers me when I have headphones in."

"I get it—wanting to be left alone. Feels better that way. Easier to avoid getting hurt." I turn to her and smile. "But then you miss out on a lot of good that comes with talking to people."

She shrugs. "Haven't met anyone worth talking to."

"You're talking to me."

She gives me another smirk. "You might be interesting. Still haven't decided, though."

"Well, you're a complete mystery to me. I know you're from Hawaii, your name means 'warrior', and I should never mess with you unless I want my arm ripped off."

"What do you want to know?"

I freeze; I didn't think she'd actually give me the chance to ask her something. I rack my brain for an interesting question, but all that comes to mind is what kind of popsicle would she be. Damn you, Meadow.

But then I remember Mr. Shadow hasn't told me anything. Maybe if I can find out why she's here, I can find out what makes her so different. "How'd you end up here?"

Kekoa's smile vanishes and I regret my question in a heartbeat. "Trying to win the bet already, huh?" I'm an idiot. Why would she want to talk about that? She's been avoiding it this whole time. Why would she want to open up to me? She's only known me for a few weeks.

But she responds. "My dad told me Mom wanted me to visit. Had a plane ticket and everything. Imagine my surprise when I land at an airport in Idaho and there's no mom. Instead there's two men there to take me to this place."

"That's screwed up."

"Yeah. So that's why I'm not too eager to get back home. He wants me here, fine. I'll stay as long as I can."

"What happened to make him send you away?"

Kekoa's chin quivers and her eyes well up before she turns away. "I learned not to let people in," she says as she takes her headphones out and puts them in her ears.

With that, Kekoa powers ahead and joins Marcus at the front. I want to chase after her, to tell her I'm sorry, that I didn't mean to pry, but there's no point. Her impenetrable wall is back up, and I have a better chance of getting Mr. Shadow to leave me alone than having a conversation with her again.

If I could, I'd cover myself in honey, lie down, and offer myself to the bears. Kekoa finally talks to me, even smiles, and I have to go and blow it. I'll be lucky if she even looks at me again. She doesn't even know I can see spectrals and she probably thinks I'm a total loser.

I spend the rest of the hike kicking myself in muted agony.

Chapter 11

I'm still so hyper focused on my complete failure with Kekoa that I don't notice the group has stopped until I almost walk into Tyler. I look up, ready for the crystal-clear pool, cascading waterfall, and a relaxing swim, but what I see is anything but beautiful.

The waterfall is nothing more than a weak stream rolling over moss-covered rocks. The pool below is a murky shade of green with light-brown foam gathering on the banks. The smell is the worst part. The initial aroma is similar to fresh-cut grass, which I don't mind, until it reaches the back of my throat and the fish odor takes over. It's like a lawn mower ran over a trout two days ago.

"This is the pool drop?" I ask, hoping they'll say no. Maybe this is just a marker to let us know we're going in the right direction.

Deacon covers his nose with his shirt. "Dude, it smells like ass. Why's it look like there's soap in the water?"

"It's a natural foam caused by rain washing decomposing plants and other organic material into the water," Tyler answers as if he's reading from the wilderness guidebook.

Marcus steps to the water's edge and takes a whiff of the suds. "There's probably a fallen tree somewhere upstream that's restricting the water flow. Could explain why the algae has been able to grow in the water, making it this color."

Something in my gut doesn't believe him. This place sounded like a perpetual paradise, not the end of a sewer drain. Not to mention there hasn't been a drop of rain since I've been here.

"You ever see this happen before?" I ask.

"It's just algae. The water's perfectly fine," Marcus tries. "Take a load off. If you guys still want to go swimming, just let us know. Shawn, can I talk to you a sec?"

We all drop our gear, but no one rushes into the pool. As the others examine the water, I try my best to listen in on Shawn and Marcus as they walk away.

"Where are the supplies?" Shawn whispers.

"You sure you told them it was today? Maybe they got the wrong date."

"They've never missed a drop and we're running short. If we don't get those supplies soon…" Shawn turns my way. I find a really interesting stick on the ground.

By the time I look back, Marcus and Shawn have moved out of range. Deciding not to push my luck, I rejoin the others. Kekoa sits in the shade of a tall tree while Tyler and Deacon tan shirtless. Only Meadow still seems excited.

"Come on, guys. It's not that bad. Algae is really good for skin care. It keeps your skin moist, conditions, and even delays wrinkles."

"Any good on scars?" Deacon jabs as Meadow lifts her sweatshirt over her head.

Tyler punches Deacon in the arm. "Dude, what the hell?"

Meadow freezes. Even though her shirt is over her face, I know that comment made it through her protective mask. It's only when I see the bare skin on the back of Meadow's left arm that I understand how low a blow that was.

Like a broken ladder, dozens of straight inch-long scars zigzag from her elbow to her shoulder. Some have aged away while others are fresh and raw. This is what Mr. Shadow has been showing me.

The shirt comes back down, hiding the cuts and revealing Meadow's smiling face. "One can only hope, right? Anyway, I think I'll try to find that bird's nest. See if the babies have hatched." She skips off along the pool's edge as if she doesn't have a care in the world.

I turn on Deacon. "What's your problem?"

"What? I'm helping her. She's gotta realize the world's not butterflies and rainbows. It sucks and the sooner she accepts it, the better she'll be for it."

My anger builds. "You don't think she already gets that? You're not helping. You're just being a bully."

"And you would know how to help her, right? You've been here for two weeks. We can't keep babying her. A little tough love is what that girl needs."

Two can play this game. "You sound just like your dad."

Deacon sits up. "How the hell would you know what my dad sounds like?"

Because I've watched him beat you every night for two weeks. "What? I thought you were a fan of tough love."

Deacon gets to his feet and starts toward me. "You don't know shit, so shut your mouth before I shut it for you."

I try to step back, but my heel snags a rock and I stumble. "All I meant was—"

Spit flies as Deacon yells, "I'm nothing like him!"

Before he can grab me, Tyler steps between us. "They'll d-d-discharge you, and if you don't complete your time, they'll send you to j-j-juvie."

So that's why he's here: court-appointed wilderness. All the reasons he could have received that verdict flash through my head, none of which bode well for me right now.

Deacon's face burns with rage, and his knuckles are white from squeezing his fists so tightly. I can see the battle within him: beat the hell out of me and go to juvie or walk away.

Finally he pushes off Tyler and points a threatening finger at me. "You compare me to my dad again, and I swear they won't find your body." With that, he storms away.

Tyler breathes a sigh of relief. "He'll calm down. You just hit a nerve."

"I got that," I say, brushing the dirt off my back. "Why's he gotta be such a douche bag?"

"It's all he knows," Kekoa chimes in from her shady spot. "He's a bully. They go after the weak ones because it makes them feel powerful."

"Someone should at least say something."

Tyler pats me on the back. "Good luck with that," he says, then heads to his tanning spot.

As I gather myself, something crashes through the woods right behind me. My first thought is that a bear is charging me as branches crack like a shotgun blast.

Meadow stumbles out of the thick underbrush. With a couple of scratches and leaves sticking to her clothes, she tries to catch her breath. Her smile is gone, and even though she's panting, she can't hide her fear.

"Jesus, Meadow. You nearly gave me a heart attack. You okay?"

"I went looking for the nest," she pants. "It's gone. Like no sign of it anywhere. I guess something could've gotten it, but then I heard this strange whispering. I thought it was one of you guys, but no one was there. I grabbed my necklace to pray, and that's when something scratched the back of my arm." She lifts her sleeve to reveal a freshly raised red line to match her old scars.

"Did you go off on your own?" Shawn asks as she and Marcus rejoin the group.

"I didn't do this," Meadow counters. "I think there's something out there."

Did Mr. Shadow do this? He's never done anything away from me as far as I know. Why would he mess with Meadow? I scan the woods, but there's no sign of the dark spectral.

"A GHOST," Marcus answers. "You know this. *A* is for what, Meadow?"

Meadow sighs. "Always partner up."

"Exactly. So let's not do that again, okay? Do you need me to check out that scratch?"

Meadow pulls her sleeve back down. "No. I'm fine."

Shawn waves the others over. "Listen up. The drop was supposed to happen this morning, but they haven't made it yet. We're a little too low in the valley for the SAT phones to reach out, so Marcus is going to head to higher ground to see what's going on. In the meantime, we'll set up here and do a little group activity."

We let out a unified groan. Marcus waves it off. "It'll be fun. You guys enjoy the serenity and the good vibes, and I'll be back with an update before you know it."

A cold spot in the bottom of my stomach starts to grow. There's something wrong with this plan. No animals or spectrals, the weird water, and now Meadow hearing things and getting scratched... Letting Marcus go off by himself, even as experienced as he is, feels like a bad idea.

"Maybe we should wait as a group," I try. "Steve and Jeremy are coming here, right?"

Shawn shakes her head. "No interaction with the outside world. That includes the transport team."

"More hypocrisy," Deacon groans. "Always partner up, but Marcus gets to go off by himself. No contact with the outside world, but you guys have walkies and can meet up with Steve and Jeremy."

"We're not in therapy," Shawn counters. That does the job and Deacon backs off.

"There could be any number of reasons why they didn't make the drop," Marcus continues. "Either way, I'll be back with answers." He reaches into his pack and pulls out his walkie. "Testing. Testing. You getting this, Shawn?"

Shawn radios back with her matching walkie. "Loud and clear. You got your beacon?"

Marcus holds up a palm-size highlighter yellow piece of tech with a white light at the top. "Fully charged and ready to go. I'll be back in a few hours. Don't have too much fun without me!" He waves goodbye and heads up into the woods.

"Don't worry. We won't," Deacon mutters.

Shawn claps her hands together. "In the meantime, let's call this base camp for now. You got ten minutes to set up your tents and meet me by the water's edge."

The seasoned pros that we are by this point, we're done in less than eight minutes. We meet up with our counselor by the water and find a small pile of gear waits for us. There's a long branch that's about five inches thick, one of our tin pots for cooking filled with green water, and a long stretch of cordage. "Listen up. This is your group activity for the day. Using only these supplies, you're going to balance that pot of water atop the end of that ten-foot log. It must stay up there for five seconds without the aid of the cord. I'll start the count when no one's touching the rope, the stick, or the pot. Good luck."

"Wait, that's it?" Tyler asks. "What's the point? You know, the takeaway at the end."

Shawn smirks. "You'll find out at the end. Get to it. We'll eat afterward." She grabs a seat against her pack in the shade and watches.

"Should be simple enough," Tyler says, examining the tools. "Just lean the stick against a tree and tie the pot—"

"Shawn said we can only use these tools, nothing else," Meadow clarifies. "No tree."

Deacon tries to pick up the log, but the thick piece of wood is heavy. He has to use both hands and a rock as a lever to get it to stand up. The top is out of our reach. "Well, unless one of you can fly, we can't just put the pot up there."

"We can tie the pot to the stick and b-b-balance it," Tyler tries again.

Deacon lets go of the log and it hits the ground hard. "You want to balance this without it falling on you, be my guest."

"You got any b-b-better ideas?" Tyler snaps.

Kekoa grabs a shady spot under a tree and starts digging. Half of me wants to join her, knowing how this is going to turn out: Deacon taking his frustration out on his favorite target.

"Come on, Ms. Perfect, this should be easy for you."

"Back off, I can't th-th-think with your incessant jabbering."

Deacon laughs. "Uh-oh, is that Tic Tyler I hear? Getting a little stressed out, are we?"

Meadow steps in. "Come on, guys. If we work together, we can figure this out."

For the next hour, all we succeed in doing is pissing each other off and dropping the log on Tyler's foot twice. Even Meadow stepped away for a minute because the constant bickering was getting under her skin. All the while, Kekoa never stops digging.

Nothing we try works. Sweat dripping down my brow, I'm ready to call it quits. The four of us sit in the shade, void of ideas. The log won't stand on its own; the cordage is about to snap; and the water keeps falling off the top.

Then, for the first time since we started, Kekoa gets up and drags the log back to the hole. After propping one end at the edge, she tries to lift the other end of the log, but she can't get it above her head.

Then it clicks for me. She's a genius! I rush to her side and help her with the log. As I lift, she turns and glares at me. At first I think she's going to tell me off and do this on her own, but instead of barking at me, she turns her focus back to the log. Good enough for me. Together we lift the log and slide it down into the hole. Then we let go and step back. With the support at the base, the log stays standing. I give it a little push and it doesn't budge.

"This counts, right?" Kekoa asks Shawn.

Shawn smiles and nods.

I turn to the others staring at us. Deacon rolls his eyes. "Where the hell were you an hour ago? A little heads-up would've been nice."

Kekoa shrugs and I see the hint of a smile under her hoodie. If I didn't know better, I'd guess she just messed with us. She then takes the cordage and ties it around a fist-size rock. Kekoa hurls the stone over a thick branch above the pole, the cord trailing behind.

Hiding my own smile, I turn to the others. "Meadow, can you fill up the pot and then Tyler can tie it to the rope?"

The two jump to action while Deacon lies back with his hands behind his head. "You guys have fun with that. Let me know how it goes."

Meadow returns with the pot full of green water as Tyler ties a knot around the handle. Kekoa hands the other end of the rope to me. With a nod from Tyler, I pull. A few drops spill out, but the pot stays tied. Thanks to Kekoa's precision, I'm able to lift the pot of water over the log then lower it onto the top. We hold our collective breath as the pot makes contact. This is as far as we've gotten in the last hour, and a growl from my stomach reminds me of what's on the line. Centered as much as possible, I slowly let go. The rope goes slack, but the pot doesn't fall. Ready to start the countdown, we stare at Shawn, who shakes her head.

"The r-r-rope," Tyler remembers. He stretches for the knot, but it's out of each. "The hole is too shallow. We'll have to take the log out and dig deeper if we're going to—"

Suddenly Tyler levitates into the air, now face-to-face with the bucket. Deacon stands underneath him, having lifted the teen up on his shoulders. "You guys can't do anything without me, can you?"

Tyler unties the knot and drops the rope.

Shawn starts the countdown. "Five…"

Deacon lowers Tyler back to the ground as the pot holds.

"Four…"

There's a chilled breeze, but not enough to move the planted log. We did it!

"Three…"

Are you having fun, Coby?

The shrill voice echoes off the inside of my skull. I feel a burst of pain behind my eyes like my head is going to split in two. My stomach clenches and I can't catch my breath. Acid fills the back of my throat.

"Two…"

Panic courses through every vein. That isn't a memory. That isn't a twisted voice from someone I know. It's Mr. Shadow. He said my name. He *talked* to me.

I scan the woods but can't see him. "Did you guys hear that?" I choke down bile as I try to focus, but my head spins and my vision blurs. I feel his icy stare on me. He's close, but where?

Kekoa raises a confused eyebrow. "Hear what?"

He's not in the woods. He's not by the water, not in the clearing… I turn to see Mr. Shadow standing behind Shawn, his tall dark figure looming over her like a tarantula stalking its prey. I try calling to her, but my voice is gone.

Something is wrong. He's different. The black static energy he's made of is more solid, like black paint dropped in clear water. I can even see a wide-brimmed hat pulled low over his face. But not low enough. An empty space filled with jagged spikes spreads wide. Too wide. Then I realize what I'm seeing.

Mr. Shadow is smiling.

Chapter 12

I stagger back, my body on autopilot. All it wants to do is create as much distance between me and that terrifying smile. My feet take me back faster and farther away until I crash into the standing log.

With a loud crack, the log snaps and the pot crashes down on my head, drenching me in green algae-filled water.

"Are you kidding me?!" Deacon shouts. I try to get up, but he pushes me back down. "What the hell, dude?"

"I…I'm sorry. I didn't mean to," I stammer. I scan for Mr. Shadow, but he's gone. "It was an accident."

"Bullshit. You did that on purpose."

Meadow tries to ward Deacon off. "Why would he do that? He just tripped. That's all. Come on. We can get it up again no problem."

Tyler holds up one half of the log. "Not like this we won't."

Before Deacon can take another go at me, Shawn steps between us. "Enough. That'll do. So what'd you guys think the point of this was?"

Deacon glares down at me, but then reaches out his hand, satisfied the task is complete. "That Cody has the coordination of a drunk gazelle."

Better than the truth. I don't want to believe it, but I can't get Mr. Shadow's smile out of my mind. And he *talked* to me. He called me by my name. A fresh shiver races down my spine.

"We learned we can't do things alone," Tyler answers. "We needed to utilize everyone in order to succeed."

"Exactly," Shawn says. "Sometimes the task in front of you seems impossible. Sometimes you're working against the odds, but you're never alone. You achieve great things when you can accept the help of others." She hands us a couple of MREs. "For coming together and fighting through adversity. Enjoy. You guys earned it."

I barely touch my food. For the rest of the meal, I scan the woods, staring into the dark corners, but there is no sign of Mr. Shadow. Why did he do that? I've gotten used to the nightly visits, the visions and whispers, but this was worse. So much worse. And his question: *Am I having fun?* Why is he doing this to me?

By the time we finish eating, the sun is setting. Even with our stomachs full, the unspoken tension is palpable. We're all worried about the same thing: when is Marcus coming back? I've even caught Shawn checking her wristwatch a couple of times.

"What's taking him so long?" Deacon grumbles. "This smell is making me sick."

"He should be back any minute," Shawn says.

I point to the walkie on her hip. "When was the last time he checked in?"

She glances at her watch again and takes a deep breath, then pulls the walkie. "Hey, Marcus. How's it going out there?" Static. We all wait, but there's no response. "Any sign of the transport team?" Again nothing. "Marcus, this is Shawn. Do you read me?"

The static fills the air around us. No one has to say anything—we know. The battery was fully charged when Marcus left, and he knows better than to hike out of radio range. If he's not responding, there's only a handful of reasons why, and none of them are good.

"The emergency beacon," I remember. "Can't you track him with that?"

From her backpack, Shawn pulls out a handheld navy-blue box with a metal antennae and a few knobs. She flips it on and the screen comes to life. A small red dot flashes on the screen.

"Looks like he's about three, three and a half clicks from here. The walkies should cover that distance fine." With a resolute huff, she throws her pack on. "I'm going to see what's going on. You five need to stay here and—"

"You're crazier than us if you think we're staying," Deacon scoffs. "Haven't you watched a single horror movie? Splitting up is the last thing you want to do. I say we all wait here for Marcus to come back."

"His marker isn't moving, and if he's not answering, I need to check on him."

"Someone should stay behind in case he comes back," Tyler says. "For all we know he could've dropped the beacon."

"It was zipped in his backpack," I counter. "There's no way he would leave that behind."

"I'm sure Marcus is fine. He knows what he's doing. Let's just wait a little longer," Meadow tries, but she doesn't sound convinced herself.

I'm outnumbered. The truth is I'm torn too. My brain wants to stay in the safety of the camp, especially because I know what's waiting in the woods. But my gut knows something is wrong. I can see Marcus walking alone, Mr. Shadow coming up behind him, lifting him off the ground...

"I'm going," I say with as much bravado as I can muster. I stand and join Shawn, but no one else moves. I try to think of a rousing speech, something to inspire them, but my mind draws a complete blank. And all I see is fear in their eyes. They know something's wrong too, but they're too scared to do anything about it.

Except for a pair of emerald eyes. "I'll go too. Marcus would do the same for any of us." Kekoa stands next to me and faces the others. "Stay here if you want, I really don't care. Just remember why you came here in the first place. What Marcus always asks us. What kind of person do you want to be?"

Tyler and Meadow exchange glances and, as if they were speaking telepathically, get up at the same time.

Realizing he's outnumbered now, Deacon takes an exasperated breath. "Whatever. But if we start getting picked off one by one by an ax-wielding hillbilly, don't say I didn't warn you."

Shawn pulls her backpack straps tight. "Fine. If we move quick, we'll be back before nightfall. Signal's coming from the north. Upstream. Let's move out." She leads the way with the tracker in hand. We fall in line, moving faster than we ever have, spurred on by both a sense of urgency and a fear of what's ahead.

As we hike up the overgrown terrain, I slide up next to Kekoa and whisper, "Thanks."

"Just keep an eye out," she says. "I bet those bright baby blues can see a lot."

I stumble over an exposed root. The way she said it—it almost seems like she knows. But how could she? I haven't told anyone; I haven't even hinted at it. "What do you mean?"

"It'll be hard to spot the beacon if it's in this underbrush."

"Oh, yeah." I take a breath. I'm just being paranoid.

Before I can say anything else, Kekoa powers ahead and joins Shawn at the front.

Meadow fills her place at my side. "I don't know how you do it, but you've really gotten her out of her shell."

"Huh?"

"Her headphones. She hasn't worn them in days. Of all the things she could've taken from home. Glad to see she's put them away."

"You brought that necklace, right? What's it mean, if you don't mind me asking?"

Meadow beams as she takes her pendant in her hand. "It protects me and gives me strength. It's a Celtic trinity knot called the 'triquetra.' It represents The Rule of Three: the mind, body, and spirit. The past, present, and future. The maiden, mother, and crone."

She points out each intricacy as she describes it to me. "The circle in it is for unity. All things coming together, a bond that can't be broken. And this is a quartz crystal. It's good for healing, but it mostly attracts, amplifies, and sends out energy. It helps me focus on the positives in my life. Still, I'm not very strong yet. There are some wiccans I've heard of that don't even need crystals; they can control their energies just by focusing."

"So you're, like, a witch?"

Meadow laughs. "I don't cast spells or fly on a broom, if that's what you're thinking. Wicca is all about promoting oneness with all that exists. The Wiccan Rede, the basis of our moral system, is 'Do what you will and harm none.' Basically, it means do good and receive it back threefold; do harm and it'll also return to you threefold. It's meant to help maintain the balance between light and dark energies."

What if I can actually see light and dark energies? Oh, and an evil one that's been haunting me most of my life is stalking us in the woods right now. "Why would you want a balance between good and evil? Why not be all good?"

"Light doesn't necessarily mean good and dark mean evil," she says. "Think of it as light being what we know and darkness is what we don't know. We're comfortable with things we are familiar with, but it's only through facing uncertainty that we really grow. Balance between light and dark just means being comfortable with the uncomfortable."

"How's that going for you?"

Meadow flashes her silver lining smile. "Work in progress. Not so good with facing my darkness. But that's what we're here for. How about you? Face your darkness yet?"

Whether I like it or not. "Something like that."

I can see Meadow debate her next words. "You know you can tell me anything right? I'm a pretty open-minded person."

"Why do you ask?"

"I don't know—it's a vibe I get from you. Like you know more than you're letting on. The way you were looking at the woods—I know you didn't trip back there. You saw something. Maybe the same thing that scratched me."

"I...I didn't see anything."

"All I'm saying is it's lonely when people don't accept you for who you are. Trust me—I know. You don't have to be alone out here. So if you did see *something*—"

"Meadow telling ghost stories again?" Deacon chirps from behind us.

"It's not ghosts," Meadow tries. "That's like seeing a leaf fall and calling it magic. There's more to it than that."

But Deacon isn't buying it. "No, it's called gravity. Simple science. This energy mumbo jumbo sounds a lot like ghosts to me."

"They said the same about gravity," Tyler says.

"Double time, you four," Shawn calls back. She and Kekoa wait at the top of a small hill. "Can't have you getting lost out here too."

We hurry along a small game trail to catch up. Even with the tracking device, I have no idea how Shawn stays oriented in these dense woods. Without her, we'd be lost. The only thing that gives me any sense of direction is the stream to the right that flows to the waterfall and back to camp.

Shawn checks the tracker; the red marker is centered on the screen. "We're here."

"Marcus?" Meadow calls out. "Where are you?"

"We're standing in the middle of a green forest in bright-orange shirts," Deacon points out. "If he was here, he'd have seen us coming a mile away."

"He c-c-could be hurt or…" Tyler stops saying what we're all thinking.

Shawn puts the tracker back in her bag. "All we know is the beacon is here. Spread out, but stay in line of sight. We've got about an hour before we're hiking back in the dark. Constant communication—I don't need any of you wandering off too."

Over the next half hour, we find a couple of empty beer cans and a plastic trash bag by the stream bank, but no beacon.

"Marcus isn't here," Deacon barks to no one in particular. "Let's just go back and—"

"Give it a break," Shawn snaps. "Would you want us to stop looking for you?"

"If it was me, I'd be dead. Tyler, you see any tracks? Any indication whatsoever that Marcus has even been here?"

Tyler shakes his head. "N-n-no, but—"

"And has anyone even stopped to think maybe the stupid tracker is defective?"

Shawn doesn't back down. "The beacon's here. Why don't you go to the stream and cool off?" Deacon wants to keep on his tirade, but Shawn insists. "That's not a request."

As Deacon heads off, I take a seat and stare at the sky, giving my eyes a break from the sea of green. Trees rustle in the breeze and clouds float by, but that's it. No birds. No spectrals…

A dark shadow blots out the sun inches above my face. "Those blue eyes of yours good for anything besides staring at the sky?" Kekoa asks.

"You haven't found it either," I snap back. The growing combination of frustration and worry is making me cranky. I take a breath. "It's worse than a needle in a haystack."

"Maybe you're just not looking hard enough."

"It's not like I have x-ray vision."

Kekoa shrugs. "It's not like the beacon's floating in the sky either."

As she steps back, the sudden sunlight blinds me for a second. I blink the colored splotches out of my vision and turn to say something snarky, but a faded neon yellow catches my eye.

I rub my eyes to make sure it wasn't from the sun. The color is still there, half buried in the mud of the streambank. It's the neon beacon.

"I found it!" I call out as I hurry to the edge of the stream. I pull the treasure from the ground as Deacon crashes into me, knocking me into the mud. I hold onto the beacon for dear life. "Dude, what the—"

I stop. He's as white as a ghost and his pupils are dilated to the size of a needle point. It's absolute terror. He mouths words, but no sound comes out. All he can do is point to the water behind me.

Chapter 13

Just below the surface, jammed under a massive boulder, are two bodies. The water is clear enough to make out details: tattoos running up and down one man's arms, a salt-and-pepper chinstrap beard on the other. Even bloated and starting to decompose, the bodies are unmistakable. We found Jeremy and Steve.

Before my brain can process what I'm doing, I'm in the water. I lean against the boulder and push. My feet slide on the slick rocks, but the damn thing won't budge. I turn to Deacon, who's still frozen in place. "Help me!"

The command snaps him out of his haze enough to get his tongue working. He shakes his head. "Dude, they're dead."

No shit. In my heart I know there's nothing I can do, but I can't just leave them like this. They're good people. They deserve better. I reach back under the water and try to lift the boulder.

"Way to go, Cody!" Tyler calls out. "How'd you see it in there?"

"I knew you'd find—" Kekoa starts, but stops as she sees me in the water trying to push a huge rock off the two men that transported each of us to this program.

Without a second's hesitation, she leaps into the water next to me.

"H-h-holy sh-sh-shit," Tyler stammers. He starts to gag and props himself against a tree to stay standing.

Kekoa locks eyes with me. "On three: One. Two. Three!"

We lift with everything we have. The jagged edge rips into my fingers as my back and legs quake from the strain, but the boulder doesn't budge.

An ear-splitting scream from the bank startles me. My grip slips. The edge of the rock tears into my palm, and a stream of red flows into the water.

Meadow stands over us, her hands over her mouth failing to mute her cry. She runs to Tyler, who's trying to keep what's left of his lunch in his stomach.

"Did you find..." Shawn stops when she sees Kekoa and me in the water with the two dead bodies of her colleagues. "Out of the water. Now."

"But it's Steve and Jeremy," is all I can get out.

"I know," Shawn states. "But right now I need everyone back down to basecamp."

Kekoa shakes her head. "We can't leave them."

"I've never seen a dead body before." With the initial shock of finding the transport team waning, Deacon stares into the water with morbid fascination. "What happened?"

"Could be anything," Shawn says. "Fallen in, got swept up by the current and pinned under the surface."

"Both of them? And they're *under* that big-ass rock," Deacon points out.

He's right. There's no way the stream's current could've forced them under. It's almost like the rocks fell on them, but we're on flat ground. One answer claws at the back of my head, sending a chill through my body, but I force it down. This can't be Mr. Shadow. As far as I know, he hasn't killed anyone since that day. He's hurt people, but only ones that were a threat to me. Why would he escalate like this?

"It doesn't matter," Shawn snaps. Even her reliable calm and composed demeanor is rattled. "Everyone back to base. Gear up for immediate evac. That's an order."

Tyler holds Meadow close, her head buried in his chest. He chokes down his gag reflex. "Looks l-l-like the f-f-foam starts h-h-here."

Tyler's right. On the opposite side of the boulder, Steve and Jeremy have created a macabre dam. Any water that makes it by them has a thin layer of brown bubbles.

Deacon shakes his head. "No one gives a shit about the stupid bubbles."

"Marcus s-s-said it came from dec-c-composing organic m-m-material, r-r-remember? That m-m-means..."

Kekoa and I realize what he's saying at the same time. We jump out, shaking as much of the water off as possible. My stomach wants to rush out my throat and run into the forest. I'm covered in that foamy water. It splashed in my face. I think I even swallowed a little...

"What about Marcus?" Meadow asks. "He was looking for them."

The mention of our missing counselor reminds me of the device still in my pocket. I hold the beacon out to Shawn. "I found this."

She grabs it and pulls a map from her backpack. Glancing at her watch, she does some quick mental calculations before marking the map. "Listen, there's nothing we can do for them now. I've noted our location, and I'll tell the authorities when we get back."

"Don't you have shit for something like this?" Deacon yells. "What about your walkie, that stupid SAT phone—anything!"

Shawn pulls both the walkie and the satellite phone from her bag. She presses buttons on each, but neither turns on. "I checked thirty minutes ago. Everything's completely drained."

"What if w-w-we took the bat-t-tteries from som-m-mething else and—"

Shawn shakes her head. "Everything's dead."

Great word choice.

"Listen, it'll be pitch-black soon, and if we don't start moving now we'll never find camp." Shawn throws her backpack on. "You can be pissed, scared, whatever later. Right now we need to pull it together and move."

"But Marcus—" Meadow squeaks.

"Is on his own. We only had the beacon to go on, and now that we have it, there's nothing we can do." She sees the worry on all our faces. "He'll be fine. If anyone can survive out here on their own, it's him." With that, Shawn heads back toward camp.

We fall in line again, somber and scared this time. No one speaks, but my mind races.

Marcus may be a world-class survivalist, but he doesn't know what's really out there. What followed me to New Beginnings. What hides in the shadows and is getting stronger with each day. Now our only connections to the outside world are buried in a stream; one of our two counselors is missing; and all forms of communication are dead. It's like we're being systematically isolated in the wilderness.

And there's nothing I can do about it. I can't stop Mr. Shadow. I don't even know what he wants. What I do know is if we don't get out of this forest soon, none of us will.

Chapter 14

By the time we reach base camp, I can just make out Shawn's silhouette twenty feet ahead of me. Like dark skeletons, the shadows stretch toward us from every direction. There's only one that terrifies me. With every step, I wait for Mr. Shadow to lunge out and snatch another one of us. But nothing happens. We return unscathed.

But something's wrong. With the fading light, it takes my eyes a second to adjust to the darkness... The fire's out. We had stoked it to last until morning. There's no way it should be out. I hurry over. Not even a glowing ember. I grab one of the black logs. Ice-cold.

Add it to the growing list of things that have died tonight.

Deacon is halfway through breaking down his tent when Shawn puts a hand on his shoulder. "We're not going anywhere tonight."

He shrugs her off. "Like hell we're not."

"We have no light. If we can't see, we'll end up lost for sure." Shawn shakes her head, "Like it or not, we're camping here for the night. Move your tents as close to the fire as possible. I want to be able to see everyone. It's a new moon, so you've got about fifteen minutes before you can't see your hand in front of your face."

Finding the right tinder is easy enough. There's been no rain, so the branches are bone-dry. Meadow and I load up two armfuls and hurry back. Tyler, Deacon, and Kekoa finish moving the tents, and Shawn has a nice circle of stones around a bundle of dried leaves and grass waiting for our wood.

Shawn stacks the smaller sticks like a teepee over her bundle. She works her magic with her flint, and a second later the camp is bathed in a much-needed warm glow.

Our tents are so close together that there's almost no room to walk between them. From my opening, I can almost reach out and touch the flames. The others are anxious, exhausted, scared... The bags under Meadow's eyes could carry a month's worth of groceries; Tyler's eyes dart around camp like a paranoid chipmunk; and even Deacon is in the process of chewing his fingernails to bloody nubs.

Kekoa sits across the fire in the opening of her tent, staring at the flames. She glances up and catches my gaze. But instead of turning away, I hold it. There's a strength there that, despite all the chaos and uncertainty, is unwavering. A look of determination that warms me more than any fire could.

"Okay, here's the plan," Shawn says from her tent. "We're taking partnered shifts tonight. Meadow with Tyler, Deacon with me, and Cody with Kekoa. Sun rises at approximately zero seven thirty, so we're doing this in three-hour shifts. If Marcus hasn't found his way back by sunup, we move out."

She reaches into her bag and pulls out the last five ready-to-eat meals. "We've got a big day tomorrow, so you'll need your energy." She puts three next to the fire and loads the other two back into her bag. "I know you probably don't feel like it, but we have to eat."

That's an understatement. Just looking at the bags makes my stomach churn. I'm afraid the second I take a bite, I'll puke everywhere. But I know I need to.

I open one of the three brown bags. Spaghetti. Usually a favorite, but right now I can't even look at it. I don't see spaghetti—I see blood-soaked intestines. There's also a packet of rice, dried fruit, saltines, cheese, an oatmeal raisin cookie, three Tootsie Rolls, and some Gatorade mix. The other two MREs are both beef stew with the same additions.

We spend the next thirty minutes forcing the food down in silence. Tyler pushes his food around and pretends to chew when Shawn turns in his direction. Deacon stuffs two of the cookies into his backpack when he thinks no one's watching. Meadow scarfs down the vegetables on her plate but doesn't touch the stew. I can hear her stomach growling from a tent over. I've barely touched my veggies, so I trade her plates. Shawn doesn't object. When Kekoa finishes her meal, she puts on her headphones and zips up the tent behind her.

Part of me wants to tell her everything's going to be okay, but I don't believe that myself.

"Time to hit the sack," Shawn says as she gathers the empty MREs. "Tyler and Meadow, you two on first shift. Deacon and I will take over in three hours. Try to get some sleep, okay?"

"Fat chance," Deacon scoffs.

I don't normally agree with him, but he's right. There's no way I'll be able to fall asleep tonight. Not knowing Steve and Jeremy are up in the stream, Marcus is still missing, and Mr. Shadow is out there waiting in the shadows.

As I'm gathering the courage to zip up my tent, Kekoa pops out of hers. She has one earbud pulled out and stares at the woods. "You guys hear that?"

"So not funny, dude," Deacon growls. "Not funny at all."

I scan shadow to shadow for any sign of what Kekoa heard, but there's nothing.

"Listen…"

"I don't hear anything," Tyler says. Meadow reaches out and takes his hand.

"Exactly," Kekoa says, stepping out of her tent, eyes never leaving the woods. "You ever heard it this quiet? No crickets, owls, bats. Nothing… Where are they?"

She's right. The eerie silence. No animals, no spectrals. I study the pool, up in the trees, and in the forest—nothing. It's like everything is hiding. There's only one thing that can scare them all away like this.

I step out of my tent to join Kekoa. She may not be able to see him, but I can.

Outside the firelight, right behind Deacon's tent, something heavy crunches in the dried fallen leaves. We all jump. The slow, methodical crunch happens again and again. Footsteps. Something big is walking around in the woods, coming closer.

"Marcus!" Meadow shouts. Hope crosses her face. The steps stop, but there's no response. "Marcus?" Meadow tries again but is less convinced.

No answer. No steps. Nothing but the eerie quiet washing over the camp again. Shawn reaches into her bag and pulls out a lime-green plastic stick. She bends it in half and a vibrant light blasts from inside. She then tosses the glow stick in the direction of the steps. It lands in the woods, casting a lime-green light on the surrounding trees…but nothing's there.

What the hell could've made that—

There's a brilliant flash of light, and I'm jamming my knee into the sternum of a bald, overweight middle-aged man, pinning him to the carpet as I rain down punches. My fists and his tank top are covered in his blood. The man's face is pulverized hamburger meat. All I feel is absolute rage. "Die you son of a bitch!"

A woman screams. "Deacon, stop! You're killing him!"

Another flash and I'm standing in a light-brown tile bathroom. I push the razor blade against the back of my arm and I feel it cut deep into my skin. The pain is dull. A warm trickle of blood flows from the incision, but I want more to pour out. With each pulse, I feel the self-hatred, the sadness, and the pain deep inside lessen. I want it all gone. Maybe if I cut deeper…

A frigid blast knocks the wind out of me and freezes my bones. I stagger back and trip over the kindling. Kekoa catches my arm before I fall into the fire. "Cody? What's wrong?"

My head is about to split in two and I can barely see straight. "He's here…"

It's never been like this before. They aren't visions anymore. It's all so real, like I'm reliving memories. I felt my fists break the man's nose and the razor cut my skin. The rage, the pain, the hurt, the hopelessness…I still feel it all.

"Who's here?" Kekoa asks. "Cody, who's here?"

Another flash and Kekoa is gone. I'm in a white waiting room with a handful of other women. I'm twisting a Planned Parenthood brochure back and forth in my sweaty grip. So many thoughts run through my mind: *What will my parents think? Am I doing the right thing? Will God ever forgive me?* Then a young, smiling nurse steps into the waiting room. "Ms. Navarro? The doctor will see you now."

I'm on my back in the middle of our camp. Kekoa is next to me, squeezing my hand while the others watch with an array of concern and fear. I try to get to my feet, but Shawn puts a forceful hand on my shoulder to keep me down.

"Cody, you okay?" Shawn asks.

"He said, 'He's here' before he passed out," Kekoa tells her.

I try to shake the cobwebs from my head. "We need to leave. Now."

Deacon steps closer, fists clenched. "What the hell's he talking about?"

Tyler tries to analyze my eyes. "Did he hit his head? Could be a c-c-concussion."

I push away, trying to focus on the woods. Part of my brain can still smell the antiseptic from the clinic's waiting room. "You don't understand. We can't stay. He's out there. Please, we need to get out of here!" I try to pull from Shawn's grip, to get everyone moving, but my body still hasn't recovered.

"Hey, asshole, who's here?" Deacon barks.

"Don't move," Shawn orders. "I'll get him a wet towel. Keep him awake." She takes the green glow stick and heads for her tent.

Meadow sits to the side, white knuckles wrapped around her triquetra pendant, praying.

"Hey, I asked you a freaking question!" Deacon moves in, ready to beat the answers out of me, but Kekoa steps in front. "Who the hell is out there?"

"You don't understand…" I try, but everything's still in a fog.

Tyler comes to my defense. "We're all on e-e-edge, Deacon. Just b-b-back off."

"Or what?" Deacon scans from Tyler to me then back to Tyler. "Oh, I get it. You got a crush, fruit loop?"

Kekoa's muscles tense. She takes a step toward Deacon, her hands clenched.

"All of you, sit your asses down!" Shawn barks with her drill sergeant voice.

Everyone freezes.

She stands on the outskirts of the tents, silhouetted by the neon-green light of the glow stick. Even with her small stature, Shawn casts an imposing aura. "We are *not* going to turn on each other, you hear me? Right now we're the only family we've got, and I won't let fear tear us apart. We're going to come together and work as one unit to get the hell out of here. At first light we'll–"

Are you having fun yet, Coby?

Mr. Shadow towers over Shawn, his wicked smile stretching out from under his wide-brim hat. Although I can't see his eyes, I know he's staring right at me.

I am.

As if pulled by an invisible string tied to the center of her spine, Shawn is ripped back and disappears into the night. The glow stick falls to the ground. Both she and Mr. Shadow are gone in the blink of an eye. There's no scream, no dragging sound, no struggle.

Shawn is swallowed by the darkness.

Chapter 15

He's got Shawn.

As I sprint through the black forest, branches rip at my face, bushes pull at my clothes, even the underbrush tries to drag me down. I didn't even realize I was running until the light from the fire had disappeared behind me.

"Shawn!"

No response. I don't know where I'm going. I have no plan even if I find her. I can't see five feet in front of me. The woods close in like they're uprooting and stalking closer, pulling me deeper into the darkness. I do the only thing I can: I keep running.

Straight ahead, I hear a sound. A muffled voice. Shawn! I dash through the dark woods. The voice is getting louder. It's just on the other side of the bushes...

I burst through a gap and run right into Tyler, who unleashes a shrill scream.

"Sh-sh-shit, dude!" he stammers as soon as he realizes it's me.

Kekoa rushes to my side. "You find her?"

How am I back at camp? I ran in a straight line after Shawn. The fire disappeared behind me, and I never turned. But here I am, on the opposite side no less. The others wait for an answer. "No, I...I couldn't see anything."

"Forg-g-get this!" Tyler grabs the glow stick Shawn dropped. "I'm g-g-getting out of h-h-here."

"Tyler, wait," Meadow tries. "We need to stay together!"

But he darts away like a rabbit hunted by an eagle. The green light bobs in the darkness until it's swallowed up.

"Have you all lost your freaking minds?" Deacon snaps. "Stop running off into the woods like a bunch of damn idiots! We need to stay here and—"

Before he can finish his thought, Tyler stumbles back into camp just off to our left.

"Wait, Tyler!" Meadow yells, but he turns and races back into the woods again.

Kekoa pulls me close so the others can't hear. "Cody, I need you to tell me right now— you know what's going on, don't you? What's happening here?"

My mouth opens and closes like a fish pulled from the ocean. I grasp at the words to explain everything, but nothing comes out. I don't even know where to start.

Tyler tumbles around a tree, this time behind us, and collapses at the edge of camp. He clutches his chest, wheezing like he's just run a marathon. "Im-m-mpossible..."

Deacon jerks the glow stick from Tyler's hand. "We need the light, so keep your dumb ass here. Listen to me…there's a bear or a tiger or—"

"There are no t-t-tigers in Idaho!" Tyler yells.

"Well, something out there got Shawn. We need to protect ourselves. We need weapons."

"Are you c-c-crazy?" Tyler screams. "We need to l-l-leave. If we can reach a r-r-river and f-f-follow it downstream, we'll find p-p-people."

Fighting back tears, Meadow squeezes her pendant and starts to pray.

Deacon gets in Tyler's face. "You want to run into the pitch-black while there's a killer bear out there, be my guest. I say we stay."

Kekoa shakes me. "Cody, who's out there? I know you can see something. You have to tell us."

"I…I can't—"

Tyler doesn't back down. "First rule of s-s-survival is to be p-p-proactive. We can't sit around and h-h-hope someone f-f-finds us. This place is two point three m-m-million acres. Without the emergency b-b-beacons, they'll never f-f-find us."

"We're being punished," Meadow mumbles. "Our anger, spite, pain—it's all coming back threefold. We did this. We—"

"You shut the hell up with that witch shit," Deacon commands. "It's an animal. That's it. There's no magic, no bad mojo, no stupid demon."

Meadow ignores him and continues to pray, which only infuriates Deacon further. He reaches down and grabs the pendant around her neck and jerks. The necklace snaps off. "Shut up!" he booms, hurling the pendant into the pool.

The second the triquetra hits the water, it feels like my entire body has been dropped into a tub of ice. A chill, deeper and colder than I've ever felt, racks my body. Every hair stands on end; my muscles cramp; and it knocks the wind out of me. I gasp for air, drowning in the cold. I try to speak, but my lips feel like they're frozen shut.

A deep, hollow wail grows from the heart of the woods. The darkness laughs. Dancing shadows from the firelight creep toward us like long disjointed fingers.

"No!" Meadow cries. "We have to get it back—"

Kekoa shoves Deacon. "What the hell was that for? She didn't do anything to you."

"I did her a favor," Deacon argues. "Maybe now she won't be completely useless."

It's already started. The fear. I can sense it; this is what Mr. Shadow wants. This is what he feeds on. And it's all my fault. I brought Mr. Shadow here.

"Meadow's right," I force out. "We need the pendant." The others may not be ready for the whole truth, but I can't sit around and do nothing. The moment that necklace fell into the water, the temperature plummeted, and a sadistic excitement radiated from the shadows. That can't be a coincidence.

"Oh, for God's sake, not you too." Deacon rolls his eyes.

But Kekoa stares at me without judgment. "You sure?"

With a nod, I struggle to stand, still feeling the weight of the cold in my bones, but everything in my gut tells me I have to get that necklace back. "Grab the rope and tie it around my waist."

Deacon throws his hands in the air. "You're all completely insane. It's a stupid rock!"

Kekoa grabs the rope, but instead of tossing it to me, she kicks off her shoes.

"What are you—no." I grab for the rope, but she pulls it away.

"I'm the best swimmer here," she says. She lifts her sweater overhead and throws it into her growing pile of clothes. For the first time, I see what's under all her baggy clothes and my mind short-circuits.

She stands there in her sports bra and underwear, and I'm frozen between turning away out of modesty and staring in admiration. Years of surfing have toned her body and sunkissed her skin. Kekoa is a marvel.

She grabs the glow stick in one hand and the rope in the other. "I'll pull on the rope three times if there's a problem. Cody?"

It takes another second for my brain to register that she's talking to me. Kekoa glares, but her cheeks flush red.

"Yeah, three times. Got it." I take the rope with both hands and hold on for dear life. There's a jerk on the rope behind me. Meadow and Tyler take hold as well.

The cold tickle of a spider crawling up my spine is all the warning I need. Shadows creep closer. I turn back to Kekoa as she approaches the murky water. "You need to hurry."

She bites down on the glow stick and, with a deep breath, dives into the freezing water. I watch as the neon green glow dives deeper and deeper. In the darkness, the eerie light illuminates the plants, rocks, and fallen trees on the pool's bottom. I try my best to not think about what she's swimming through right now.

A tightness swells in my chest, and I realize I'm holding my breath too. How long can she stay down there? Will she even be able to find the pendant? I try to force out the negative. She's got this. She has to. For all our sakes.

The fire is down to embers, its lifeforce drained by the closing night. Mr. Shadow is close. We need to move faster.

Then the neon-green glow starts to rise. Higher and higher until Kekoa breaks through the surface and takes a lungful of fresh air. "I got it!" she calls to us from the middle of the pool, her arm raised triumphantly with a chain hanging from between her fingers.

A warm relief washes over me as Kekoa covers the distance in a few strokes. As I reach to help her from the water, I see that wide terrible smile. At first, I think it's a reflection. Mr. Shadow is behind me. But I'm wrong. So wrong. He's not behind me; he's below Kekoa.

"Kekoa!" I yell, but it's too late. She's jerked hard under the water.

"*No!*" I scream as I watch her disappear into the darkness, arms still reaching for me. The rope rips through my hands and snakes into the water.

I dive after her. Although the cold instantly drains the life from my muscles, I swim deeper, chasing after the fading green light.

You did this, Cody. They all know this is your fault.

I ignore Mr. Shadow's voice in my head. I ignore the pain. I ignore everything except the green light. I swim and swim, clawing for that light. For Kekoa.

The green light rests at the bottom of the pool. A few more kicks and I see her. Kekoa floats there like a marionette. Her long raven hair flows around her face. Her eyes are open, but it's a blank stare.

I'm too late.

Chapter 16

No! You can't have her!

My lungs scream for air. My fingers are numb. My vision closes in around me. But I don't care. I grab Kekoa by the wrist, plant my feet on the rocky bottom, and launch us toward the surface.

The orange glow of the campfire beckons us. I drag her to the light, but the frigid murky depths drain me with each kick. My body is failing. I'm slowing down. The light is fading. I'm not going to make it.

Before my vision goes dark, my head bursts through the surface. Hands grab me and Kekoa and drag us out of the water. Gasping but alive, I collapse on the bank.

"She's not breathing!" Meadow cries. "Someone do something!"

Tyler kneels next to her and interlocks his fingers over her chest, but freezes. His eyes are wide and his arms shake uncontrollably.

I cough out a gallon of water and grab his hand. "You can do this. Save her."

"W-w-what if I do it wr-r-rong? What if I m-m-mess up? What if—"

I look him in the eye. "She's dead if you don't!"

Although Tyler's hands continue to shake, he turns his attention back to Kekoa. "First, ch-ch-check for breathing. Place your ear next to the mouth and n-n-nose and check to see if the victim's chest is moving." Tyler mirrors each step as he flies through CPR 101. "No movement. Next, check for a p-p-pulse."

Deacon stands over us, staring down at Kekoa. "She's freaking blue, man. Hurry up!"

Tyler presses his fingers to Kekoa's throat. "No pulse. Start compressions. Place the heel of one hand in the center of the chest, interlock fingers, and push down two inches. Thirty compressions at a rate of one hundred per minute. One, two, three…"

Tyler leans into each compression, caving Kekoa's rib cage. On the third, there's a deep crack. He keeps going. "CPR often leads to broken ribs. Do not stop. Nineteen, twenty…"

Deacon paces back and forth. "Dude, she's dead. What was that? What happened?"

Ignoring him, Tyler turns to me. "Cody, kneel next to the victim's head." I hurry over and follow his lead. "To open the airway, tilt the head back and lift the chin. Pinch the victim's nose closed then cover the victim's mouth with yours to create an airtight seal and give two one-second breaths. Make sure the chest rises and falls."

I follow his instructions to the letter. She's ice cold. I count in my head and breathe out. Thousand one.

Her chest rises a few inches. I breathe out again. Thousand two.

"Continue this cycle until emergency help arrives," Tyler narrates as he continues compressions. "One, two, three, four..."

"What emergency help?" Deacon shouts. "We can't call anyone."

Meadow grabs Kekoa's hand and holds it tightly. "Come on, Kekoa. Come back to us."

"Nine, ten, eleven..."

A fountain of water bursts from her mouth. Tyler rolls her onto her side and another stream of foam and water pours from her lungs. It takes Kekoa a minute to purge most of the lake onto the ground next to her and catch her breath. With a wince, she holds her injured ribs and leans up onto an elbow. Her eyes dart to the water's edge and she pulls her feet a little farther away.

I offer a hand to help her to her feet. "You're safe now." Her eyes linger on the water for a second longer before she takes my hand and slowly lifts herself to her feet.

"You did it! You're amazing, Tyler!" Meadow tackles him with a powerful hug. "That was the bravest thing I've ever seen."

Deacon has his hands on his head and his jaw on the ground. "Holy shit. Holy shit!"

Kekoa opens her clenched fist to reveal the quartz triquetra pendant and offers it to Meadow. "I think you dropped this."

Meadow accepts the gift like a mother cradling her newborn. Her eyes well up as she puts the necklace back on. "Thank you."

"All that for a stupid necklace? Really?" Deacon grumbles. I know that's the closest to an apology we'll get, but I'm too cold to care. My teeth are chattering like a machine gun.

Tyler leads us to the campfire. "Get them some dry clothes. We've got about ten minutes before hypothermia sets in." With that, everyone snaps into action. Even Deacon helps Tyler get us close to the fire while Meadow grabs towels and a change of clothes.

Within minutes, Kekoa and I are wrapped up tight next to the warm fire.

Tyler comes back with a handful of extra tinder. "You good?"

I nod. "Yeah. We're good."

"Tyler?" Kekoa adds. "Thanks for, you know, saving my life."

Tyler blushes. He sits next to Meadow, who pulls him in close for another tight hug.

"Either of you mind explaining what the hell's going on?" Deacon asks.

Although I knew this question was coming, I don't want to answer it. I don't even know where to start. I'm physically, mentally, and emotionally exhausted; I don't even know what time it is. All I want to do is curl up in a ball next to the fire and pass out for the next week.

"I...I don't know."

"Bullshit. You know something. Why'd you need that necklace back? Who is this 'he' you keep saying is here? Who's out there? Who took Shawn? Answer me!"

"Back off, Deacon," Kekoa warns, but I cut her off.

"I...I have schizophrenia. That's why I'm here. Things get worse when I get stressed. I guess I just had an episode or something."

"People with that disorder may suffer from hallucinations," Tyler adds. "Are you seeing or hearing things?"

"Both," I admit, keeping the truth and the lie as close together as possible. Most people tend to stop asking questions after I tell them this, but Tyler isn't like most people.

"Like what?"

Deacon throws his hands in the air. "Great. So we're lost in the middle of the woods with a psycho off his meds?"

"That's enough," Kekoa orders. "It's late. We're all running on empty and need to get some sleep."

"What about Shawn?" Deacon protests. "If you think I'm going to sleep after—"

"The plan hasn't changed," Kekoa continues. "At first light, we head out to get help. Cody and I still need to warm up, so we'll take the first shift. The rest of you, get some sleep."

Deacon looks like he wants to argue more, but exhaustion gets the better of him. "Hopefully no one else disappears tonight," he grumbles as he crawls into his tent.

Meadow holds Tyler close. "I don't want to be alone tonight. Can I stay with Tyler?"

Kekoa glances at me and shrugs. "I'm not in charge... Sure, I guess."

"If either of you has slurred speech, memory loss, severe shivering, or if the shivering suddenly stops, wake me up," Tyler orders.

I smile. "Yes, sir, Dr. Pung."

The two head off to Tyler's tent, leaving me and Kekoa alone by the fire. I feel her gaze on me, but I'm afraid to look. She must have a thousand questions racing through her head. And I have my own for her. How does she know I can see things? Does she know what I can see? Why hasn't she told the others? Why is she protecting me?

But I turn anyway and, for the first time, really see her face. Her long wet hair cascades down her right shoulder, and her green eyes stand in stark contrast to her olive skin. The firelight dances across her face, giving her a golden aura.

She raises her dark eyebrows and gives a little smile. "You okay?"

"What?" I shake my head and turn my attention to the fire.

"You were staring."

"No, I wasn't." I poke the fire with a log to be a little more convincing. "Are you okay? Tyler thinks he may have broken one of your ribs when…"

She watches me for a second before allowing my weak attempt to divert the focus to succeed. "Yeah. A little sore, but I'm fine. Thanks to you."

I don't know how to respond. Thanks to me? She wouldn't have even needed saving if it weren't for me. They were all getting along fine—then I show up with Mr. Shadow, and it all falls apart. Shawn, Marcus, Steve, Jeremy… If I didn't come here, none of this would've happened.

Cold, wet hair drapes down my shoulder, snapping me out of my self-deprecating train of thought. Kekoa rests her head on me. I freeze, unsure of what to do and scared to move.

"I'm here when you're ready."

It is such a simple statement, so matter of fact, but I know what she's saying. I know the weight behind it, and it means the world to me. There's no pressure, no expectation, no judgment. She knows something—maybe everything—but is letting me talk about it in my own time. She's offering her help, not demanding it. No one's ever done that before.

But I don't want to ruin the moment. So we just sit there, Kekoa's head resting on my shoulder, and stare at the fire.

Chapter 17

The airy whine of a harmonica wakes me from my dreamless sleep. I don't remember getting into my sleeping bag, let alone falling asleep. I peek outside my tent to see the sun rise over the horizon. A cool breeze welcomes me, and I shake the cobwebs from my head.

Then a chill hits me in the chest. Marcus's harmonica woke me up. I listen for it again, but the music is gone.

There's no Marcus with his harmonica preparing squirrel or rabbit stew. There's just Deacon snoring next to a smoldering fire.

Meadow pokes her head out from the tent next to me, eyes wide with hope. "Marcus?"

"You heard it too?"

"We b-b-both did." Tyler unzips the tent the rest of the way. He and Meadow climb out and scan camp like a pair of prairie dogs.

Tyler rubs his disheveled hair. "Could've been the w-w-wind. That p-p-plus our unc-c-conscious expectations of m-m-music with first light could th-th-theoretically—"

"Oh, my God, it's too early for your shit. Just shut up," Deacon mumbles.

Kekoa steps out of her tent. "It wasn't the wind or a group hallucination and it wasn't Marcus."

She pierces me with her green eyes. I know what she wants me to do, but things are bad enough. I shake my head, trying my best to telepathically tell her now is not the time.

"Nope," Deacon, now alert, shakes his head. "It's too early for this shit too. I'm not hearing this. Not out here. Not like this."

"You're not scared, are you, Deacon?" Meadow pokes.

Deacon pumps up his bravado. "Pfft. Please. Whatever. It doesn't matter. Ghosts don't even exist."

"We d-d-don't know that f-f-for certain," Tyler protests.

"Don't tell me, you, Mr. Scientific Method, believe in ghosts? Show me a shred of proof that they are out there, and I'll carry Meadow out of here on my back."

"What y-y-you're asking is a logical fallacy. One can neither prove nor disprove something doesn't exist, because the absence of evidence is not evidence of absence."

I agree with Deacon—it's too early for this. We stare at Tyler with blank expressions.

Tyler takes a breath, trying to think of an easier way to explain it. "Let's say for a-a-argument's sake that

Cody here is c-c-color blind. He may not be able to s-s-see color, but that's not evidence that color d-d-doesn't exist."

"I'm already sorry I said anything," Deacon waves him off. "Listen, I think I know what's going on. They're testing us."

I wish that were true, but I know better. "Seriously? After all you've seen—"

"Think about it," Deacon continues. "What *have* we seen? Two bodies? Did anyone check if they were even real? Kekoa could have gotten her foot caught on something. Shawn disappearing into the woods is easy with no light. Maybe she's with Marcus. The music this morning could've been a recording. They're probably watching us right now."

"Why w-w-would they do th-th-that?"

"To see if we're really ready to go home," Deacon answers. "Put us under stress and see what happens. They already have us alone in the woods—they could do all sorts of weird psychological experiments on us and no one would know. It makes sense."

As much as I want to argue with him, I see the hope in Meadow and Tyler. Both are ready to break, and the truth is, right now, we all need something to hold on to. Maybe believing it's all some elaborate experiment is best. Either way, as long as we stay together, Mr. Shadow should leave us alone.

Kekoa walks into the middle of camp with Shawn's backpack and pours all the gear out. "It doesn't change our plan. We still need to get out of here. Now that we can actually see, let's take stock of what we've got and double-check every battery. Maybe we'll get lucky and have enough juice for a call."

After a half hour, we've divided all the gear into piles: clothes, electronics, medical equipment, food, and survival tools.

Kekoa sits in the middle of it all. "There's good news and there's bad news. The good news is we've got a lot of cool stuff. We have a multipurpose knife, flare gun, a dozen emergency glow sticks, lighter, duct tape, fishing line, fire steel, a compass, and a map. Should make surviving out here a little easier."

"And the bad?" Meadow asks.

"The bad is the meds are locked and the key is gone; every battery is completely drained; and there are only two ready-to-eat meals left."

"Still think this is a test?" I ask Deacon.

"They leave exactly everything we need to survive and make it out of here? Yeah, I do."

"We sh-sh-should eat," Tyler says. "Load up on en-n-nergy and head out. Worst case s-s-scenario, if we don't m-m-make it out by nightfall, I'll set t-t-traps and Meadow can collect any edibles n-n-nearby."

Deacon shakes his head. "I still vote for staying here. It's the last place they told home base we'd be, so when no one checks in, this is the first place they'll look. We need to secure our camp, build a perimeter, make some weapons—"

Tyler takes an exasperated breath. "This isn't *L-L-Lord of the Flies*. Basic survival states the f-f-fastest way to reach civilization when lost in the woods is to follow a river downstream."

"That won't necessarily work," Kekoa argues. We all turn to her, surprised that someone would debate Tyler on his facts. "There are tons of streams out here that come from underground reservoirs that lead to nowhere."

"So we stay?" I ask.

"No. We know there's a town west of here, but we still need to get to higher ground and assess where exactly we are. Then we can make a better decision."

She stares at Deacon, waiting for a retort. He makes the wise choice and stays quiet. Kekoa continues, "Meadow and Tyler, break down camp; I'll take care of the food; Deacon and Cody, pack up the gear. We should get moving before the sun gets too high."

No one moves, caught off guard by Kekoa's commanding presence. I think she's even surprised herself because she turns to me for a little help.

"You heard her—let's get going," I say, grabbing some of the gear and loading it into my backpack. The others head off to their respective duties. Kekoa smiles.

I really like that smile…

As I finish packing the survival gear into our bags, I see Deacon sitting in the dirt with the locked box of meds in his hands. He turns it over and over.

"Deacon, you good?"

He shakes his head, lost in thought. "It's all our meds…" He trails off. There's no smile, no excitement. He seems worried. "Cody, I…I need you to take these."

"But it's locked."

"Just take them," he snaps, then throws the box at me. "I'm not screwing this up." He gets up and walks away. There's still a decent amount of gear left to load up, but I let him go. I get it—a lot may have changed overnight for us, but why we're here hasn't. We still have our own inner demons to battle.

I don't know how Marcus and Shawn could hike every day with all this extra weight and not complain. I'd distributed Shawn's gear among the five of us. At first, I barely felt the extra pounds. But after hiking uphill for hours, my legs are on fire and I'm pouring sweat. The others aren't faring much better. Even Deacon, always trying to get a workout in, struggles.

To distract myself from my cramping muscles, I try to spot any animals or spectrals, but there's nothing. The silence is the most unnerving. It's like every living creature in the forest has vanished. Not even a single insect. All I hear is the rustle of a breeze through the trees and the crunch of our footfalls.

I'm not the only one who notices. Meadow examines the trees. "It's so quiet. Where are all the birds?"

"There are studies on the disappearances of m-m-migratory animals," Tyler says. "Climate change, drought, t-t-toxins, real estate development, h-h-habitat destruction—"

"Does it really look like there's been any construction around here?" Deacon points out. "They could be sensing a predator nearby and have gone into hiding." He catches a few of us staring at him. "What? *Shark Week* is the shit."

"But what kind of predator would make the entire forest disappear?" Meadow wonders.

Mr. Shadow.

Ahead, Kekoa stops. "Check this out."

We reach a clearing and stare in absolute awe. We're on a large rock jutting out into space and, beyond that, a massive panorama of the entire Payette National Forest. Wisps of white clouds brush across the blue sky, and deep valleys cut through the vibrant green hills. The distant snowcapped mountains give the majestic view an imposing backdrop.

Deacon groans. "Anyone see a town? How about a building? Roads? Cars? Any sign of freaking life at all?"

Just like that, the gorgeous view turns into a daunting realization. There's nothing out there. Just an endless wilderness. I turn to Kekoa. "Please tell us this isn't west."

She drops her backpack with an exhausted grunt. "Let's take a thirty-minute break. See if there's anything we can grab for lunch." Kekoa walks to the edge of the rock and takes a seat, her legs dangling off the edge.

A unified sigh escapes our lips as we let our gear fall from our backs. My lower back is killing me, and all I want to do is sit down in the shade and take a power nap.

"Cody, can I talk to you for a sec?" Kekoa waves me over.

The nap can wait.

Standing on the edge, I see just how high up we are. There's nothing but air between me and the rocky ground hundreds of feet below. My head spins and the rock feels like it's made of wet tile. I sit down next to her before vertigo gets the better of me.

"So this, uh, doesn't bother you?"

Kekoa smiles. "This rock's been here for hundreds of thousands of years. Been through earthquakes, storms, and fires. I don't think us standing on it is going to move it."

A tall shadow appears behind us, and for a second I swear Mr. Shadow has come to push us off the ledge. "Time for some sun," Deacon says. He takes off his shirt and lies down on the rock. "You guys don't mind, right?"

I fight the urge to throw him over the edge when Tyler hustles over. "You are so thick," he barks, grabbing Deacon by the arm. "Can't you see they w-w-want to be a-a-alone?"

"What?" I watch the little hamster in the wheel of his brain start running. "Oh. Ohhhh! Gotcha. My bad." Deacon smirks. He winks at me and slaps my shoulder, nearly knocking me off balance, before Tyler drags him away.

With those two heading off into the woods, I turn to Kekoa and my mind goes blank. I've never been great at talking to girls, and now here I am in a picturesque location with the most gorgeous girl I've ever seen wanting to talk to me, and I'm frozen. As she stares at me with those green eyes, I struggle to come up with any cohesive words. "So the weather's nice at least."

Are you kidding me?! The weather? I should just jump...

"For now." Kekoa nods to the left, where ominous clouds are gathering on the horizon. "That's coming this way. We need to make it to the cabin by nightfall."

The forest below is an endless expanse of green. "What cabin?"

She points off to the right. "You see that small area with no trees? There's a tiny brown triangle in the middle. My bet is someone cleared the trees to build a hunting cabin."

"You bet? What if there's no cabin?"

"Then tonight's going to suck." She sighs. "'The future is worth it. All the pain. All the tears. The future is worth the fight.'"

Where have I heard that before? Did a psychologist say it to me? A teacher? Maybe one of those inspirational quotes they hang up on a wall with a photo of some remote location or wild animal. I rack my brain, trying to remember why that phrase seems so familiar.

Then my jaw drops. I know where... "Did you just quote *Martian Manhunter*?"

"Don't judge. J'onn J'onzz is the best. Super strength, speed, flight, and he can also phase shift, shapeshift, and is telepathic."

"But he's scared of fire. Light a match and he's in trouble."

"That's the best part! Superman's only weakness is kryptonite, but he overcomes it by giving just a little more effort. Every. Time. J'onn J'onzz's weakness is real and has a purpose. He watched his family die in a fire. It doesn't cripple him physically—it breaks his heart.

That's why he says, 'The future is worth the fight.' He knows what real pain is, but he keeps going."

"Fair enough," I concede. "But Batman could still take him."

Kekoa rolls her eyes. "Of course you like Batman."

"What's that supposed to mean?"

"Really? A kid whose life is shaped by trauma and fear learns to harness it and uses it against the evil that goes bump in the night."

I shrug. "He has no powers but still beat the entire Justice League single-handedly."

Kekoa shakes her head and giggles. It's the closest I've heard to a genuine laugh. Her smile makes her eyes squint and the two dimples come back in the corner of her cheeks. I can't help but smile back.

With her feet dangling over the cliff's edge, she leans back. Her hand rests next to mine. I feel the charge between our fingers. All I want is to reach out and hold her...

Kekoa takes a deep breath and her smile falters. "My mom's favorite was Zatanna. She'd tell me Zatanna was such a powerful magician because she knew there was more to this world than just what we could see. There was an entire other plane of existence, and Zatanna could tap into that and control it. That's what made her so strong."

The last time Kekoa's mom came up in conversation, I messed it up. I tread these waters carefully. "We don't have to talk about your mom if you don't want to."

"It's actually why I wanted to talk to you. My mom…saw the world differently than everyone else. The island knew her as the local crazy lady, always making up these stories about the things she saw. She called them '*uhane*.' It means ghost or spirit."

My lungs catch in my throat. "What was she like?"

"A badass. The island is harsh to outsiders. I got into a lot of fights at school. My parents argued a lot too. No one believed her. But she never wavered. The last time I saw her, I was sleeping and she came into my room. I woke up because the hinges creaked, but I pretended to be asleep. She came in and kissed my forehead. Before she walked out, she just stood there and watched me. I wanted to roll over, to tell her good night, but I didn't move. The next day she was gone. I was seven."

Kekoa turns to me, her eyes glistening. She rubs them before any tears can fall. "I've never told anyone that before. Not even Shawn."

"Why me?"

"I don't know, maybe because you remind me of her." Kekoa's hand inches toward mine. "I wasn't there for my mom. I don't want to do that again. Cody, I want you to know you can tell me the truth. I'll listen. Just trust—"

Our fingers touch and my head explodes. In a searing flash of light, I'm ripped from the rock and find myself sitting around a bonfire on a tropical beach at sunset. All my classmates party on the sand, celebrating Olivia's sixteenth birthday. She sits opposite me with her arms around her boyfriend, the two sharing a laugh at something he just said.

"Hey, Kekoa. Thought I'd get you something." Noah hands me a red Solo cup and takes a seat next to me. Always so thoughtful. Noah's such a good friend.

Another flash. My head swims in a thick cloud and my legs are made of Jell-O. I know what drunk feels like, but this is something different. I can't control my body. I watch Olivia take her boyfriend to the water, leaving me with Noah. He helps me to my feet. "You don't look so good. How about we go somewhere and rest?"

He leads me to his car. From behind, a garbled voice calls, "Noah, what's up with Kekoa? She good?"

Noah waves back. "Just had too much to drink. I'm taking her home."

Noah rests me in the backseat, then gets in the front and drives away. With every bump, every turn, my body shakes, but I'm a ragdoll. I shake and shake and...

Kekoa, eyes wide with fear, grips my shoulders and shakes me. "Cody?! Holy shit, what the hell was that? Are you okay?"

I choke down the bile forcing its way up my throat. It takes me a second to remember where I am. The vision was so real. It wasn't just a memory—I was there; I was Kekoa.

"Who's Noah?" I ask, still groggy from the experience.

Kekoa pulls back like I just electrocuted her. "Where'd you hear that name?"

"There was a bonfire—"

Kekoa jumps to her feet. "No! Tell me now, where did you hear that name?"

The last time I saw her like this, she nearly ripped Deacon's arm off. "I'm sorry! I didn't mean to, it's... It hasn't happened with you before, so I thought..." I don't know what to do. Her eyes are wide with anger, so I instinctively reach out to help her. Wrong move.

"Don't touch me!"

I pull back. "Yeah. Okay. I'm sorry –"

"'I'm sorry' doesn't even begin to..." Kekoa points a menacing finger at me. "Don't say another word. Forget that name, you hear me? And stay the fuck away from me!" She pushes past me, leaving me alone on the rock ledge.

Behind us, the others race over. "You guys okay? We h-h-heard yelling."

Kekoa throws up her hoodie and grabs her gear. Ignoring them, she stuffs her earbuds back in and starts down the hill alone.

"There's a cabin at the base of this mountain," I say, trying to take the focus off Kekoa. "We need to hurry, though. Bad weather's on the way."

We grab our gear and head after Kekoa, who's already a distant body darting in and out of our line of sight. We have to jog to catch up.

Along the way, Deacon comes up next to me. "That went well."

"Not in the mood, Deacon."

"Take it from a guy who's pissed off more girls than I'd care to admit. Let her cool down and give her some space. When she doesn't want to murder you in your sleep, apologize. Just make sure you mean it. Chicks can tell when you're full of shit."

The problem is I don't think Kekoa will ever calm down. I just experienced her deepest, darkest secret without her permission. I violated her memories. The rage on her face was real and violent. I wouldn't be surprised if she never talks to me again.

Everyone I know, everyone I come in contact with, I end up hurting. If I disappeared into the woods, the others could escape. This is happening because of me. If I just left…

A hand on my shoulder snaps me out of it. Meadow smiles. "Hey, it's okay. She'll come around. Friends always do." A distant clap of thunder echoes over the trees. "Come on. We'd better hurry."

Friends. Something I've never been too familiar with, yet I feel some connection to this group of social outcasts. Could I actually leave them? I guess we really are in this together.

We slip and slide down the side of the mountain, using tree branches and bushes as support. Another rumble of thunder. The storm's getting closer. Hopefully we can make it to the cabin in time.

If there even is a cabin.

Chapter 18

We made it to the bottom of the mountain by the time the rain hit. A wall of frigid water crashed down on us like someone had turned on a massive shower at full blast.

The New Beginnings orange parkas do little to keep any of us from getting soaked. Mine covers to my knees, exposing everything below. Deacon has it the worst: with his tall frame, the parka barely reaches his hips. On him, it's more like a water-repellent shirt.

Twenty minutes later and we still haven't found the cabin. My teeth rattle so hard it feels like they're going to shatter in my mouth.

Over the downpour, Deacon yells, "Are we there yet?"

Kekoa powers forward without glancing back. Either she didn't hear him or, more likely, doesn't care to respond. She hasn't said a word since the incident on the mountaintop.

Tyler, with Meadow wrapped under one arm, walks next to me. I don't know if his stutter is from the cold or his nerves, but it's worse than ever. "We n-n-need to find sh-sh-shelter soon or we're all gonna be at s-s-serious r-r-risk for hypoth-th-thermia." He nods in the direction of Kekoa at the front. "Are you s-s-sure we're g-g-going the right w-w-way?"

"She knows what she's doing," I try to convince him, even though I don't believe it myself. But at this point what options do we really have?

Meadow pokes her head out from under her parka. "Where'd Kekoa go?"

I shield my eyes from the curtain of rain, but Kekoa is nowhere to be seen. "Kekoa!"

No, not again. Not after what I did. I take off, the others right behind me. "Kekoa!" I scream, but the rain drowns me out. Although it stings my eyes and bites at my exposed skin, I race forward blindly.

Ahead, an orange parka flaps in the wind, but as we get closer, something is wrong.

There's no Kekoa. Her parka is snagged on a low branch and whips back and forth. I pull it down and my heart sinks.

The parka rips from my grip. A soaked Kekoa, breathing heavily, wraps herself back up. "I tried signaling you, but the wind took it."

At the sight of her, relief floods my body. She's okay. All I want to do is wrap my arms around her, but sensing this, Kekoa steps back, not even looking at me.

"Why were you s-s-signaling us?" Tyler asks, breaking the awkward tension.

Kekoa nods behind her. "Found the cabin."

We follow her to a single-story wood cabin, a glorious haven, in the center of a small clearing. We hurry to the front porch awning to get out of the torrential downpour.

Deacon scrutinizes the porch. "Bet you New Beginnings rigged this place up with some hidden cameras for their experiment. Could even be using this place as their home base."

Tyler peers in through one of the side windows. "D-d-doubt it. Doesn't l-l-look like anyone's b-b-been here for a w-w-while."

Meadow tries the door, but no luck. "Maybe there's a key under a rock or something."

Deacon picks up one of the stones with a destructive grin. "Or the rock is the key."

Tyler waves him off. "I've g-g-got a better i-i-idea." He reaches into his backpack and pulls out the meds folder. He flips through the pages and pulls out two paper clips.

"You know how to pick a lock?" I ask.

Tyler bends the paper clips until he's happy with the new shapes. He then kneels in front of the lock and gets to work. "Parents k-k-kept the good l-l-liquor locked away. There was a cute s-s-senior I was trying to im-m-mpress. One q-q-quick Google search and I w-w-was in. My p-p-parents still don't know the v-v-vodka bottles are f-f-full of water."

There's an audible click, and Tyler stands with a proud smile. Deacon wraps an arm around him. "I knew there was a glitter-coated rebel in there somewhere."

"Let's j-j-just get in and warm up," Tyler says. As he turns the handle, the door slides open with a long, low creak from the rusted hinges. One by one we filter in.

The rain crashing down on the roof echoes through the large open space. I try the light switch. Nothing. Maybe there's a generator or something, but I keep my hope at bay.

A massive floral rug protects the living room floor. It's flanked on either side by a long leather couch and two matching chairs. A couple of fishing poles lean against the wall next to me, and on the far side is a stone fireplace with an elk head mounted above it. Its empty black eyes stare at me like an unwelcomed guest, so I turn my attention to the photos on the walls.

Most are of a family of five spending time in the great outdoors. Dad is a huntsman. There are a few photos of him and his teenage son in camouflage with their bows and arrows. The action shots are of the mom and two younger daughters cliff jumping or dirt bike racing. I stop at one of the whole family, arm in arm, in front of this cabin. They all seem so happy.

"I don't know about you all, but I'm starving," Deacon states, snapping me out of my trance. He heads for the kitchen. "Let's see what we got in here."

Tyler heads for the fireplace. "I'll get the fire going." Meadow follows.

That leaves Kekoa and me. Now's my chance to apologize. To make her understand I have no control over what Mr. Shadow shows me. To make her *believe me*.

But before I can get a word out, she disappears down the hall. Her cold shoulder is worse than the biting rain. I have half a mind to chase after her, but I don't. Instead I follow Deacon through the door to the kitchen.

It's a quaint space. Pots and pans hang over a center island that doubles as a kitchen table with a couple of stools around it. An old-school iron stove is on the far side with a rack of spices and a one-pound bag of salt next to it. There are also two doors. The one to the left of the stove leads to the back of the cabin, and the second is next to the refrigerator. I'm guessing it's either a pantry or leads to a cellar.

Deacon digs through the stainless-steel refrigerator. "How is there not a single bite to eat in this entire place?" He slams the door shut.

"They probably took it with them. Didn't want bears or people breaking in and eating all their stuff. You check in there?"

Deacon turns to the door next to the fridge. "The cellar? It's pitch-black. Can't see shit."

I'm about to let it go when my stomach lets out an audible roar. I've been starving since we left the top of the mountain. All this exercise and stress just make it worse. Whether or not I like it, we need more than just the two remaining MREs.

"I'll get us some glow sticks," I say, heading back into the living room. Meadow and Tyler try to coax a small ember to life, but they're struggling.

"We need kin-n-ndling," Tyler says.

I dig through my backpack to get to the glow sticks and pull out my sketchbook. We could use this, but there's something I want to save first. It takes a second, but I find the page I'm looking for: Kekoa and the sparrow spectral.

I tear it out, fold it up, and find a safe place for it in my bag. The rest I toss to Tyler. "Here, use this."

"We couldn't," Meadow says.

"It's okay. Get that fire started. Deacon and I are going to check out the cellar for some food."

Meadow reaches for the crystal pendant. "You should take this…just in case."

Part of me wants to take her up on the offer, but they need it more than I do. I can at least see what's coming for us. "Thanks, but we'll be fine."

I return to the kitchen and join Deacon at the cellar door. "You sure you want to do this?"

Deacon takes a glow stick. "We need food. Let's just make it quick."

After we crack the sticks, the green glow illuminates the top of the stairs. A few steps down and it's total darkness. An instant chill races up my spine. I want to slam the door shut, lock it, slide every piece of furniture I can in front of it, then burn the cabin down. If Mr. Shadow had a happy place, this would be it.

Then the smell hits. I gag. It takes all my willpower to keep my stomach down. It's like someone used cheap perfume to cover up a pile of rotting meat. I hold my shirt over my nose.

Deacon tosses his glow stick down the stairs. It lands a dozen steps away. The green glow brings shape and substance to the corner at the bottom of the stairs, but nothing more.

He steps aside. "After you."

With his light at the base of the stairs, the visibility cuts into the fear but doesn't eliminate it. I hold my glow stick out like a shield, half expecting black talons to reach up, grab me by the ankle, and rip me into the darkness.

The wooden stair creaks under my weight, but nothing happens. I take another step and a hand falls on my shoulder. I jump out of my skin. Deacon laughs. "Gotcha."

Dick. We head down the stairs. Luckily the smell doesn't get worse as we go lower. At the bottom, he picks up his glow stick. I turn the corner and hold mine out.

The space below the cabin is more storage than anything else. There are stacks of old toys, boxes covered in dust, shelves of gardening equipment, and tons of other junk. This family's motto is definitely: "It's better to have and not need than to need and not have."

I shine my light over boxes full of broken Fourth of July decorations and see a large black-and-yellow piece of equipment. I let out a sigh of relief. "Found the generator."

"Fire that baby up."

Please have fuel, please have fuel, please have fuel.

I wrap my fingers around the rip cord and pull. The generator rumbles, but nothing catches. I try again, pulling harder. The engine struggles then catches. Above, a lone bulb flashes to life, bathing us in welcomed light.

I instantly regret turning the power on. I now know where the smell is coming from. Dozens of dead animals. Heads mounted on the walls, stuffed bodies strewn across the space, skins hanging from the ceiling. It's like a taxidermist and a psychopath gave birth to an interior designer.

"At least we have power," Deacon tries, staring at the macabre scene around him. "And check it out—we got food!" He pushes over more boxes as he makes his way to a steel shelving unit on the side wall with canned food on it. "Finally some good news."

I work my way over to him. We just need to grab the food and get the hell out of here.

I'm so focused on the rows of canned food that I slam my leg into a large white freezer. Maybe there's more food in here. I try to lift the top, but it's locked. The metal latch on the side is down, but where a small padlock should be, there's a thin beaded chain with an orange key.

I know that key. It opens the med kit. Shawn kept it around her neck…

My mind screams to leave, to get out of the cellar, get out of the cabin, and never stop running, but my fingers work on autopilot. I unclip the chain necklace and pocket the key. I can't stop myself from opening the lid.

Dark red paints the white interior. Mangled limbs, mutilated organs, and two eviscerated torsos dressed in orange shirts fill the freezer. Sitting on top of all this carnage, staring up at me with milky-white eyes, are the decapitated heads of Shawn and Marcus.

Welcome to my home, Coby.

I snap around. Mr. Shadow stands at the foot of the stairs. His massive black figure fills the frame, but I can only stare at his wicked smile. The cellar door slams shut and the single light bulb explodes, casting us back into darkness.

Chapter 19

"We need to go!" I shout to Deacon. My eyes struggle to adjust to the dying green light.

Deacon stumbles into a pile of boxes, dropping a few of the cans of food he's carrying. "What the shit, dude? Turn the light back on."

"He's here. We need to get out of this cabin." I don't have time to explain further. I don't even know if I can. I hurdle a wooden rocking horse, grab Deacon by the shoulder, and drag him toward the stairs. I don't see Mr. Shadow; I don't know if that's a good or a really bad thing.

Deacon tries to pull back. "It's just a power surge or something."

A combination of fear and adrenaline gives me an iron grip. I pull him up the stairs, taking two at a time. I make it to the door and try the handle, but it's locked.

"Hey, man. This isn't cool. Stop playing."

"I'm not. It's locked." I pound on the door and call out at the top of my lungs, "Tyler! Meadow! We're in the cellar. Open the door!"

Why don't you just stay and play? For old-time's sake.

His voice is like a spider crawling inside my skull. I slam the door with my shoulder, but the damn thing doesn't budge. I hit it again and again until my shoulder is about to shatter.

"Don't you hear that?!"

"You about to dislocate your shoulder? Yeah." Deacon shoves me aside. "You gotta kick it like this." He turns his back to the door and grabs the handrail for support. He lifts his leg and kicks back like an angry horse. His foot makes contact right next to the knob and the door crashes open with a splintering of wood.

I dive into the kitchen, pulling Deacon with me, and slam the door behind us. It doesn't matter that the lock no longer works. Anything to create distance between Mr. Shadow and us.

Tyler and Meadow run around the corner. "You two okay? It sounded like something—"

"Everyone needs to get out. Now!" I scramble to my feet and race for the front door. Kekoa hurries down the hall on high alert.

"I don't know… The light went out and he just lost it," Deacon explains behind me as I reach the door. I nearly rip it off the hinges as I throw it open. I don't care that it's still a monsoon outside—anywhere is better than in this slaughterhouse.

My feet can't gain any traction in the mud, but that doesn't stop me. The rot of the cellar clings to the back of my throat. Behind me, the others stand on the porch, just short of the rain.

"We need to leave. We can't stay here. It's not safe! *Please!*" My heart is pounding through my chest, and I can't catch my breath. Images of the freezer flash through my head. Of Shawn and Marcus. Their mangled bodies. The way Shawn's hair was matted with wet blood and Marcus's right eye was swollen shut like it was winking at me. I feel the bile in my stomach touch the back of my tongue.

"Cody, stop!" Kekoa's eyes are filled with concern. "What's going on? Did you see something?"

"He's here," I pant. "I saw him in the basement with—"

"Who's here? Who are you talking about?"

"Mr. Shadow!" I scream. "You need to get away. Now!"

"Who the hell's Mr. Shadow?" Deacon says, stepping next to Kekoa. "No one else was down there, dude."

"You can't see him. No one can, except me. He killed them. He killed everyone." They don't believe me. I see it in their eyes. But it doesn't matter, they just have to go. "Shawn and Marcus are in a freezer in the cellar! We have to leave!"

"Bullshit." Deacon turns to Kekoa. "Cellar's full of dead animals. Probably just another scare tactic to test us. Or Cody's been off his meds for too long and his crazy's kicking in."

Tyler shakes his head. "Cody, you n-n-need to come in. It c-c-could be a combination of exposure and hypothermia. You're not th-th-thinking straight."

They don't believe you. Do you want them to? I can make them believe.

It's like hot tar dripping in my ears. "He's here! Please, you have to believe me!" I'm on my knees in the mud, begging. But no one's listening. I want to cry, scream, run, drag them away, but I can't move. I don't know what to do.

Kekoa scans the surrounding woods. "Where is he, Cody? Where is Mr. Shadow?"

"I don't know. I can't see him right now." It's hopeless. They won't believe me until it's too late.

She takes a tentative step out into the rain and reaches out to me. "Then we're safe right now, right? Come on, take my hand. Let's get inside and figure out—"

She stops in her tracks. Her mouth is open midsentence, hand reaching for me, eyes wide, but she's frozen. She's just staring at me.

No, not at me. Above me. Then her hand begins to shake.

The rain...I can't feel it. It's still pouring around me but not on me. Whatever she's staring at is blocking the downpour. What I do feel is the frigid touch of a thousand spider legs crawling up my spine.

"What the hell?" Deacon asks. The others stare behind me, brows furrowed in confusion.

"Cody...get away from there," Meadow squeaks out.

But I don't. Instead I fight the stiff muscles in my neck and creak my head around to see what's behind me.

There he is. Mr. Shadow. But he's no longer a black mass. He stands behind me nearly corporeal, his face hidden behind his wide-brim hat, his long obsidian trench coat draped over his wiry frame. Two bony hands with impossibly long, talon-like fingers are interlocked in front of his chest as if he's waiting patiently in line.

Then his head snaps with a jolt and his neck crooks at a most unnatural angle. For the first time, I can see his face. Mr. Shadow's skin is pulled tight, showing every curve of the bones beneath, accentuating his sunken obsidian eyes. His mouth contorts into that horrifying grin that stretches the length of his face, showing jagged rows of rotting teeth.

Hello, Cody.

Before I can stumble back, his hand darts forward, his crooked fingers wrapping around my throat. His grip is like burning ice. My feet leave the ground as he lifts me with ease.

I wanted to thank you for inviting me here...

I claw at the frozen hold that's squeezing tighter around my throat, choking the air out of me. Suddenly there's a flash. I see the broken, bloodied remains of Meadow, Tyler, Deacon, and Kekoa strewn around the cabin. Their blood splattered all over the floor, the walls, the ceiling.

Thanks to you, I have met such interesting people...

There's another flash. Mom's mangled body lies in a pool of blood in our living room.

We have such a delightful future together...

Kaylee and Haylee cower on the bottom bunk in our room, screaming as Mr. Shadow looms over them. I watch from my bed, tied down by invisible chains. "Don't touch them, you bastard! Leave my sisters alone!" He reaches out for them and—

A burst of white light fills the room. Mr. Shadow unleashes a blood-curdling screech and the vision vanishes. I'm back in the woods under the pouring rain.

Mr. Shadow releases his death grip, and I fall to the muddy grass, gasping, filling my lungs with the cold air. A hand wraps around my wrist. Meadow pulls me back toward the cabin, holding out her pendant with the quartz crystal like a shield.

"Come on, Cody. I can't keep it back. We need to go before—"

Mr. Shadow slams Meadow with a powerful backhand, sending her cartwheeling through the air. She lands with a sickening crunch at the foot of the cabin. The crystal pendant flies from her grasp and slides into the mud.

Shaking the haze from my mind, I scramble to my feet. "Get inside!" I scream, slipping and sliding in the mud on my way back to the cabin. Kekoa and Tyler brave the rain, each grabbing an arm of Meadow's still body. Deacon holds the door as they drag her inside.

Mr. Shadow roars again, but I don't turn back. All I can focus on is getting through the open door. I rush to the front porch and tackle Deacon, sending us sprawling into the cabin.

I turn back to see Mr. Shadow standing at the edge of the woods, staring at me. His smile has vanished and his black eyes are filled with absolute rage. He opens his ragged mouth wide and screams at the top of his lungs, quaking the cabin. Then he charges, flying over the muck and the mud with supernatural speed.

Untangling myself from Deacon, I lunge for the door. I try to force it shut, but the howling wind is too strong.

Kekoa slams into the door next to me. With our combined strength, we force the door shut just as Mr. Shadow crashes into it.

The impact sends Kekoa and me flying back, hitting the floor hard. The entire cabin shakes like a bomb went off. Mr. Shadow pounds on the door, the wood cracking and splintering. The hinges buckle with each massive strike.

"We have to barricade the door!" I shout, racing for the couch. Kekoa helps slide it over. Deacon shoves a large wooden armoire over and topples it onto the couch.

We stand back and watch Mr. Shadow's strikes rattle the barricade. Then, just as the door is about to burst in, the pounding stops. Everything goes silent.

"Is it g-g-gone?" Tyler asks.

Isn't this fun, Cody?

I close my eyes and cover my ears, trying in vain to block him out. It's like he's standing right next to me, whispering in my ears.

Kekoa puts a hand on my shoulder. "Cody, what's going on?"

I am going to take them. One by one. I will make them scream. I will make them suffer.

"You can't hear him?"

Kekoa shakes her head.

Just like the two in the cellar, until you're the only one left. There's nothing you can do to stop me.

A shiver runs down the side of my neck. I turn and see his demented face staring at me through a window. "What do you want from me?!"

I want your pain, your sorrow, your fear. I want your power. I want to survive.

Mr. Shadow fades back into the darkness. I run to the window, but the woods are too dark and the rain too heavy to see anything. He's disappeared.

I turn to the others. Kekoa leans against a wall panting heavily; Deacon stares at the front door with his fists clenched. Tyler kneels next to an unmoving Meadow. "Tyler, is she—"

He shakes his head. "Just un-n-nconscious. B-B-But her leg…"

Meadow's left foot is bent at a horrible angle. "Can you fix it?"

"She needs s-s-surgery. I c-c-can maybe—"

"What the *fuck* was that?!" Deacon erupts. "You all saw that shit, right?" He turns his wild eyes on me. "You. You knew that—whatever it is—was out there, didn't you?"

He slams me against the wall. Fear and anger contort his face into something I've only seen in visions. He looks just like his father.

"That was Mr. Shadow, wasn't it? Wasn't it?! That's the thing you were warning us about. Tell me or I swear I'll—" He pulls his fist back, ready to bash my skull in, when Kekoa grabs his arm.

"Enough," she commands. "Right now we need to block any other way that thing can get in. We can settle this after."

As much as he wants to pummel the life out of me, Deacon's self-preservation comes first. For good measure, he slams me against the wall before letting me go. "We're not done. Not by a long shot," he threatens before storming out of the room.

Without another word, Kekoa turns to follow. "Thanks," I call out, stopping her.

She turns on me, and for a second I think she's going to pick up where Deacon left off, but she takes a deep breath. "You should've warned us."

She walks away. I turn to Tyler, but his attention is on Meadow.

"The med case is in my bag," I say, tossing Tyler the key. "See if there's anything in there that can help."

Tyler catches it. "I th-th-thought the k-k-key was with…" The realization washes the rest of the color from his face. "They're r-r-really in the c-c-cellar, aren't th-th-they?"

All I can do is nod.

Chapter 20

We pull up loose floorboards to board the windows. Kekoa uses a mallet she found in a kitchen drawer, while Deacon and I grab spare logs from the fireplace to drive in the nails. We stack mattresses against the remaining doors and burn through every inch of duct tape from Shawn's backpack. As we secure the house, Tyler fashions a splint for Meadow's leg from a broken broom. After thirty minutes of frantic lifting, shoving, pulling, and hammering, the cabin is transformed into a makeshift fortress.

I hope it's enough.

We sit around the fire, our only source of light and warmth, draped in some blankets Kekoa found in the back bedroom.

The group huddles while I sit opposite them, trying to hide behind my own safety blanket. Their eyes dart in my direction, but as soon as I make eye contact, they turn away. The tension in the air feels like Mr. Shadow's grip on my throat.

Meadow's hazel eyes are glazed over in a drug-induced haze. "I knew spirits were real. The rain was like falling on nothing, but there was something. It made the most spectacular silhouette—"

"There was nothing spectacular about it," Deacon snaps. He turns on me, his anger holding strong. "So how about it, Cody? You mind telling us *exactly* what the hell that thing is?"

"I call him Mr. Shadow," I croak. My throat is still sore from having my life nearly squeezed out of me. "He's a spectral."

"S-s-spectral? You mean a g-g-ghost?"

I shrug. "Honestly, I don't know."

"What does it want with us?" Deacon presses.

"I don't know."

"Why can we see it now?"

"I don't know."

"Are there others like it?"

I look to Kekoa for help, but she won't meet my gaze. "I don't—"

"You don't know. Yeah, we got that," Deacon barks. "Is there anything you actually do know or are you just useless?"

"I know he killed my dad in front of me," I snap. That stops Deacon, but it's too late for me. The dam breaks. I can no longer hold back the torrent. "I know he's been haunting me ever since. I know I have nightmares every night. I know my mom thinks I'm crazy. I know he's hurt people. I know he can see things—people's darkest secrets. I know because he tells me. I know he's changed since I've been here. He's different. Stronger. He's actually *talking* to me now. I know he's a monster and I know no one believes me."

"I believe you," Kekoa says, staring at me. "I believe you, Cody. You said he can see things. Is that how you knew about…"

I wipe a tear and nod, knowing what she's referring to. "I'm so sorry. I can't stop it."

Deacon throws his hands in the air. "I call bullshit. This thing, Mr. Shadow, shows you people's secrets? How about our secrets, Cody? What do you know about me?"

"You d-d-don't need to s-s-say anything," Tyler tries, but Deacon shuts him up.

"Yeah, he does. You want me to believe all this crazy talk, tell me something."

"You were in your little brother's room when you tried to beat your dad to death." That shuts Deacon up. "The only reason you stopped is because your mom lay on top of him. You tell everyone you wish you killed him, but you really wish he was a normal dad you could play catch with. I've felt Meadow's razor blades cut the back of my arm and tasted the bile Tyler threw up after his parents screamed at him for liking a boy."

I turn to Kekoa. She holds my gaze, stoic. As much as I want to turn away, to hide in shame, I don't. I owe her; I owe them all an apology. Her most of all.

"Mr. Shadow showed me everything. I didn't want to say anything because…because I had no right to know. I'm so sorry. I'm sorry for invading your privacy, for bringing Mr. Shadow, for doing this to you all. If it weren't for me, none of this would've happened."

No one speaks for a while. The others sit in silence, processing everything I've said. All I can do now is prepare for the worst. Will they kick me out? Send me into the wilderness to face Mr. Shadow on my own? Will they lock me in the basement and run for their lives? If I'm gone, would Mr. Shadow leave too?

A small voice breaks through the silence. "You couldn't have known that stuff about Mr. Shadow, about how he would change the way he did." Meadow tries her best to smile through the pain meds. "This isn't your fault."

"Ch-ch-change... That's it!" Tyler exclaims. "There's a v-v-variable. Change only occurs when a variable is a-a-added to the equation. S-s-something happened; something *changed*. Y-y-you said it yourself. So the question is 'W-w-what's the variable?' What's making Mr. Sh-sh-shadow change?"

"You guys are buying this?" Deacon scoffs. "Freaking ghosts and visions and magical powers. What a load of crap. I get Meadow falling for it, but Tyler, there's no way a science nerd like you can actually believe this."

"It doesn't sound m-m-magical. More ph-ph-physiological than anything else. There's evidence of s-s-senses being heightened—sharks smelling a drop of blood over miles of ocean, bats using echolocation to see at night. Maybe Cody can do something s-s-similar."

"Or they're testing us," Deacon tries. "It still makes the most sense. They could have spiked the water at the pool to make us hallucinate, used some sort of high-tech equipment to make someone invisible, and are filming this whole thing as some crazy social experiment."

Tyler shakes his head. "Occam's Razor: the s-s-simplest answer is usually the r-r-right one. Do I believe New Beginnings has fabricated a test where we discover f-f-fake dead bodies, our counselors vanish, we experience a m-m-mass hallucination, and an invisible f-f-force attacks Cody and breaks Meadow's leg with no one coming to h-h-help, or do I believe something I can't see is h-h-hunting us? As terrifying as that realization might be, it's the simplest and checks all the b-b-boxes."

As much as Deacon wants to argue, it makes sense, even to him. "Okay, fine," he acquiesces. "Let's say Mr. Shadow is legit. What does he want?"

I rack my brain, then remember the last thing he said to me. "He said he wants my fear. My power. He wants to survive. But I have no idea what that means."

We all sit in silence for a minute. For all the years he's followed me, I've never asked myself what he wanted. I assumed he was haunting me, enjoying the torment, giving himself a moment of distraction in his eternal purgatory. But now he's coming after me, after us. If he *wants* something…why me? What could I possibly have that he wants?

"It's us," Meadow whispers. "He wants us."

"How many painkillers did you give her?" Deacon huffs. "Cody says Mr. Shadow or whatever has been with him since he was a kid. We just met. Your timeline is off."

Meadow ignores him and continues. "Cody, Mr. Shadow's name is actually super accurate. In Wicca we call evil spirits 'shadows.' They exist in a parallel world to ours and feed on energy. There are three kinds. The first is like a leech; you won't notice if one or two are attached to you, but if too many latch on, you're in trouble. The next is bigger, like a vulture; if you're not careful with your energy, they can pick you clean."

"But what about mine?"

"I think Mr. Shadow is the last one. They love to feed on the life energy of humans. And they're super smart. They try to trick you into feeding them, or if you resist, they can even enter your body and feast. They're insatiable."

Tyler leans forward. "What you're describing sounds a lot like a d-d-demon."

Meadow gives a quick nod. "Pretty much. Yeah."

"So I've had a freaking demon following me for the last ten years? Why?"

Meadow shrugs. "Your energy. If you can see him, you must have a different energy, something he's probably never tasted before. I bet when you and your dad showed up, he couldn't resist."

"A demon addict. Great." Deacon rubs his temples.

"But this still doesn't s-s-solve for the variable," Tyler continues. "What has c-c-caused Mr. Shadow to change?"

Meadow opens her hands. "I already told you: it's us. Think, Cody—besides here, has there been a time when Mr. Shadow has gotten worse?"

I feel the gears move in my mind but not fast enough. It's like a blurry image is coming into focus, and

I'm starting to get the picture. "My last seventy-two-hour hold, I started getting night terrors, but they weren't my dreams. I was in the other patients' nightmares controlled by Mr. Shadow. He was making the entire ward relieve their trauma and forcing me into a front-row seat."

Meadow nods. "Think of how much negative energy he was able to feed on there in only three days. The more he consumes, the stronger he gets."

"The night terrors stopped about a week after I got home..." The final piece comes together. "Because he was around only me again. When I left, I cut him off. He's been out here for weeks with us."

Deacon leans forward. "So you gave an addict a shot of the good stuff then took it away? That's why all this shit is happening. We're his fix." Deacon shakes his head and stifles a laugh. "Oh, man, we're so screwed."

A horrible thought hits me like a sledgehammer. Everything Mr. Shadow's done—the nightmares, the voices, nearly killing my classmates—it's all been to get me here. To get me back with others in just as much pain, with just as many negative emotions. He's been manipulating everything to get me here.

Tyler looks like he's working through a tough math problem in his head. He mumbles to himself before taking an exasperated breath. "It doesn't make sense. We have the e-e-equation, but there's no solution. What's Mr. Shadow's endgame? If we stay on our current trajectory, our expected survivability drops with each passing day. What's he going to f-f-feed on when we—"

"I know what Mr. Shadow wants." It all makes sense now. Bringing me here, killing the counselors, isolating us, feeding, and now the others can see him too. "Before this all started, he was a shadow only I could see. Now I can see his body; I can see his face; and you saw his silhouette. I think he wants to be whole."

Meadow shakes her head. "If a demon took on a physical form, that would be bad. Like your-worst-nightmare-come-to-life, walking-death, end-of-the-world bad... We can't let that happen. We have to stop him."

Deacon laughs. "You're all crazy, talking about demons and energies and shit. Tyler, you want a simple answer for this? I got one for you: get rid of Cody. No more Cody, no more Mr. Shadow, no more problem."

The solution catches everyone off guard. I've thought about leaving, but the way Deacon said it? Get rid of me? Does he really mean what I think he means?

"You can't seriously be thinking about killing Cody, are you?" Meadow asks.

Deacon snorts. "What? No. Give him some rations and water, point him in the right direction, and hope the door doesn't hit him on the way out." He turns to me and shrugs. "Sorry, but I'm not about to die for you."

"We can't just send him into the woods like that. It's a death sentence," Meadow pleads. "Besides, there's no guarantee Mr. Shadow will leave with Cody."

"He left a psych ward full of crazy kids. He's going to leave the four of us."

"Cody stays." Kekoa's simple statement startles me. "He's the only one who can see Mr. Shadow. Whether we like it or not, until we figure out what to do, Cody's our only chance of surviving this. We need him."

I can't get a read on her. As much as I want to believe Kekoa just saved me out of the goodness of her heart, there's a distance between us. Maybe she didn't do it for me. Maybe she did it to protect herself. It's the most rational choice: keep around the one person who can see the danger. I don't know what hurts more: Deacon wanting to get rid of me or Kekoa keeping me around as a safety precaution.

Meadow throws off her blanket, frantically scanning the floor and checking her pockets. "My pendant—where's my triquetra?!"

"Are you seriously worried about your stupid necklace?" Deacon laughs. "With everything you just heard, *that's* what you're thinking about?"

Meadow is nearly in tears. "It can protect us. The quartz crystal channels energy."

As crazy as it sounds, it clicks for me. "That's why I was able to get Kekoa out of the water, and when I was being choked, you ran at Mr. Shadow. You had the necklace…"

An image of the crystal pendant landing in the mud flashes through my mind. When Mr. Shadow hit her, the necklace flew from her grip. I didn't even think to grab it. "It's in the mud."

Deacon waves us off. "Well, we can kiss that goodbye. No way in hell are we going out there with a damn shadow demon thing stalking us."

"Since Meadow is the only expert here on this stuff, if she says we need it, then we need it," I argue. "It doesn't matter if I can see Mr. Shadow or not if we don't have a way to protect ourselves. That crystal may be the only thing we have that works. Without it, we're defenseless."

"How do you p-p-propose we get it b-b-back?"

Deacon turns to me with a wicked smirk and my heart plummets. "We don't. He does."

Chapter 21

I'm a scuba diver wearing a swimsuit of dead fish thrown into shark-infested waters without a cage. When Deacon slams the front door shut behind me, an audible click lets me know I am stuck out here. Alone and exposed. I turn to see everyone watching through the gaps in the floorboard barricade.

Tyler gives me a half-hearted thumbs-up. "You g-g-got this."

There wasn't much of a debate about me going by myself. Meadow tried to come up with another plan, one that didn't involve a sacrificial lamb, but no one volunteered. Logically it made sense to Tyler—I'm the only one who knows where the necklace is and I can see Mr. Shadow; anyone else would be a liability. Kekoa sat against the wall with her headphones on and hoodie up. So Deacon marched me to the door and sent me on my merry way.

The rain continues to pour. Even with limited visibility, the woods feel darker. I need to hurry and find that pendant. The last thing I want is to be trapped out here in the darkness with Mr. Shadow on the hunt.

I scan the empty spaces of the woods for any sign of Mr. Shadow. Nothing. Part of me is relieved, but my baser instincts scream, *He's out there, watching, planning.* But I have one job to do; get the necklace. The longer I'm exposed, the worse my chances are of making it back.

I take a deep breath to steady my resolve. Here goes everything…

My shoes hit the mud and slide a few feet before gaining traction. I dash to the spot where I remember the pendant landing, a couple of yards from the front door. After sliding to a stop, I dig my hands into the soft earth, trying to rake my fingers over the necklace. With all this rain, there's a good chance it got buried. I just pray it hasn't washed away. I rummage through the mud but come up empty, then sweep wide around me. I swear it landed here. It has to be here! Unless...

You didn't think it would be that easy, did you? You're better than that, Cody.

I fall hard on my tailbone. Mr. Shadow towers over me in the dark rain. All I can see is his skeleton face and sinister smile under the wide brim of his black hat.

I want to play a game.

His death-rattle voice sends shivers through my bones. "I don't give a shit what you want," I scream. "Just leave us alone!"

If you want the necklace, you must play. You know the game: Hot/Cold.

He's mocking me. Taking the game I play with my sisters, the game we love, and twisting it into something demented and evil.

I'll even give you your five questions.

The last thing I want to do is play a game with this psychotic demon, but if he has the necklace, I have to play.

"How do I know you're even telling the truth?"

I have never lied to you—unlike everyone else you've ever known.

I get to my feet. At least if Mr. Shadow focuses his attention on me, the others will be safe.

Oh, and you'll have one minute to find it and bring it back. If you don't, you'll get to watch me hang your friends' heads over the mantel.

"That's bullshit," I yell. "How am I supposed to find—"

59...58...57...

I hear the countdown like rusted fishing hooks digging into the inside of my eardrum.

Okay, think! I play this game with Kaylee and Haylee all the time, what do I need to do first? I need to know which direction the necklace is in. Right now it could be anywhere. I need to cut this in half.

I take a step forward. "Am I hotter or colder?"

Interesting move. Are you sure–

"Just answer the question!"

Colder.

Okay, so it's behind me. That cuts half of the woods out. Not bad for one step, but that still leaves the other half. I need to cut it again. I take a step to my left.

"Hotter or colder?"

Hotter. You won't find it one step at a time, Cody.

I ignore the grating sandpaper. Picturing the cabin from a bird's-eye view, I mentally cross out everything in front and to the right. That leaves the southwest quadrant.

52...51...50...

It can be anywhere. Miles away or buried or hanging from a tree.

I jump up and grab part of the wooden overhang. My feet dangle just off the ground. Please don't be a wasted question. "Hotter or colder?"

Clever boy. You really are quite good at this. Neither.

I drop down with a shred of relief. If Mr. Shadow had said colder, the pendant would have been on the ground or even buried. If he had been warmer, it would be hanging, possibly so high I would never have a chance. But since it didn't change, that can only mean one thing: the pendant is at eye level.

That's three, Cody. You only have two more, and you haven't even started looking.

My mind races. All I can think about is the ticking clock and what will happen to my friends once it reaches zero. There's still way too much space; I need to know where it ends.

An idea pops into my head, but it's risky.

I have to run past the pendant. If I go far enough and Mr. Shadow tells me I'm colder, I'll know the area to look in. But if he says hotter, I've lost a question and, more important, time.

Time's wasting. 43...42...41...

Without another second of hesitation, I take off at a full sprint. I know if I run directly southwest, I'll be cutting the possible space in half. But I can't run for too long because even if I find the pendant, I won't make it back in time. Not only that, but I also need time to search for it.

So while I run, I count ten seconds in my head. That makes twenty seconds total of running, which gives me a twenty-second window to find the necklace. I hit the woods at three seconds. I race past trees, leap over bushes, and dodge branches as best I can.

As soon as I hit ten in my head, I slide to a stop, then turn to the cabin to see if Mr. Shadow followed me. He's gone.

Halfway there. It's not looking good for your friends, Coby.

I swing around, and there he is, smiling down at me with his harrowing grin. Moment of truth. "Hotter or colder?"

Mr. Shadow hesitates for a second, but it feels like an eternity.

Colder.

As much as I want to celebrate this small victory, I haven't won anything if I can't find the pendant. But at least I now know it's within reach.

Last question. Better make it count.

I do the only thing I can—I take a step to the right. "Hotter or colder?"

Hotter. That's it. No more questions. 27, 26...

I race back through the woods, scanning every tree, branch, and bush for any sign of the pendant. The rain isn't helping, but the canopy cover is keeping the worst of it at bay. With the five questions, I've got the space down to a fraction of what it was, but there's still so much ground to cover.

And the whole time, Mr. Shadow counts down.

19, 18, 17... Who should go first? Meadow? Too easy. What about Deacon?

"Shut up!" I scream. "I can't think. I can't—"

15, 14...

I hurdle a fallen tree and my feet land on a dry patch of dirt. I've found a small beaten path. It curves into the woods to my right, but the left has a direct path right back to the cabin. This must be where the homeowners walk in and out from. If that's the case, this path could lead us home.

A small twinkle catches my eye.

The quartz triquetra necklace hangs like a Christmas ornament over the path. I found it!

Slipping and sliding in the mud, I run with everything I have left. I lunge forward and wrap my fingers around the prize. I stuff the necklace into my back pocket. Now I just have to get to the others and—

"Hey, buddy."

A bolt of lightning strikes my chest. There, standing in front of me, is Dad. He looks just like he did the day we went camping. Happy, healthy, and alive.

"Dad?" This isn't real. There's no way...

He smiles, making his electric-blue eyes squint. "You found the necklace. Well done! Now take it and run. Run home, Cody, and never look back."

"What—what are you talking about?"

Dad kneels next to me. "You have to protect Mom. Protect your sisters. This path will take you home. If you go now, you'll survive."

I stare down the beaten path—my road to my freedom. I can leave all this behind and get back to my family. I can be done with this hell. Could it be that easy?

"What about the others?"

"They sent you out here to die. You owe them nothing. You've seen who they are, what they've done. They're here because their families are better off without them. Leave with the necklace and you'll be safe. Haylee and Kaylee will be safe. You can be normal. Isn't that what you want?"

I see it. Mom relaxing on the back porch, watching me play with the twins in our yard. The air is filled with laughter and joy. There's no shadow looming over me, no secrets, no lies, just a happy family spending time together.

I have a normal life.

But at what cost? I see the cabin behind Dad. Inside, my friends are depending on me to come back. If I leave, they'll have no way of protecting themselves. Mr. Shadow will kill them all.

"Do the right thing: protect your family."

I glance down at the road home. The way back to my mom and sisters. I hope they'll understand. I hope they'll forgive me.

I turn back to my dad. "I'm sorry, but I'm not normal; I'm special. You taught me that. And I *am* protecting my family."

My dad is lifted off the ground. He claws at his neck, trying to pull away the force that's holding him in the air. His blue eyes stare at me, filled with panic.

Not again. "Dad!" I race to his side and wrap my arms around his legs. I try to lift him, to loosen the hold on his neck, but he keeps choking. As I try to save him, the choking sound turns to sick, metallic laughter.

I step back, and my dad is laughing. But it's not his laugh. It's Mr. Shadow's.

I watch in horror as my dad's neck snaps to the side with a nauseating crack. He swings below the branch, hanging by an invisible rope. His body decays with years of rot spreading across his skin. His electric-blue eyes turn a milky white.

Dad's mouth moves, but it's Mr. Shadow's voice that comes out. *So be it. Oh, by the way. 6...5...*

No…it was a distraction. He was wasting my time.

I sprint by my hanging dad and down the path. The mud pulls at my shoes. Roots grab for my feet. Branches claw at my face. Even the wilderness tries to hold me back.

I know the math: I gave myself ten seconds. There are less than five. I won't make it.

3... The cabin comes into full view.

2... I break through the treeline.

1...

I crash full speed into the side of the cabin. A shooting pain rockets down my arm as I collapse to the ground. My ears ring and everything's a little blurry, but I lift myself to my feet.

"I made it," I yell at the wind. "I made it…" I try to spot that evil smile, but I can't find Mr. Shadow. I pound on the door. "Let me in!" I shout. "I've got the necklace."

A bloodcurdling scream rips through the walls. I peer through the side window. Deacon flies across the living room and crashes into a table. He lies there, unmoving, his eyes wide open and blood pooling under him.

"No! I made it. Leave them alone!"

Meadow tries to hobble down the hall, but Mr. Shadow is right behind her. He grabs her by the back of the neck and lifts her. She screams as Tyler charges, but he's caught across the jaw with a powerful backhand. Blood splatters against the window as Tyler slumps to the ground. Mr. Shadow wraps his long fingers around Meadow's head and twists. Her neck spins all the way around and her cries are cut short.

"Cody!" Kekoa calls from the kitchen.

I race around the cabin to a boarded-up window. Kekoa stands on the other side, eyes wild with terror. "Oh, God, Cody. Please get me out of here! He's coming. I don't want to die."

Scanning for anything I can use to shatter the window, I grab the largest rock I can find. "Get back!" I slam the rock against the window and it explodes, raining shards of glass into the kitchen. Using the rock to break away the rest of the jagged pieces, I clear enough space to grab the floorboards.

I push and pull as hard as I can, but the floorboards won't budge. Kekoa tries to help, but nothing works. The nails hold strong.

I punch the boards. My fists crack and bleed, leaving red streaks across the old wood until one cracks. As Kekoa pulls, I punch it one last time and it splits in half. One more and there should be enough space to crawl out.

There's nothing you can do now, Cody. She's mine.

Kekoa grabs my hand. "Please. Don't let him take me..."

"Just look at me, Kekoa. I've got you. Just a little more—"

Mr. Shadow appears behind her, his malicious smile grows wider.

There's a sickening tear, the sound of a pumpkin's innards being scraped out with a spoon, and Kekoa's hands fall from the wood.

Her deep-green eyes plead for help. Blood drips from the corner of her mouth. "Cody?"

I reach through the gap for her, but just before my fingers can wrap around her hand, she's jerked back and disappears into the darkness.

Chapter 22

"*No!*"

I kick as hard as I can at the remaining floorboard. There's an audible crack, so I load up and put all my weight into the next kick. My foot makes solid contact with the floorboard, and with the full force of my strength, fear, and anger behind it, the board splinters.

I crawl through the window and crash onto the cabin floor.

"Kekoa!"

As I scramble to my feet, footsteps race through the cabin. My fear of Mr. Shadow is gone, replaced with absolute rage. I grab one of the floorboards with two rusted nails sticking out the end, ready to destroy whatever's charging me.

The steps turn the corner and come to the door. White-knuckled, I load up and swing.

The nails slam into the wall inches above raven hair peeking out from under a hoodie. "Jesus, Cody."

I release the impaled floorboard and wrap my arms around Kekoa. She's alive!

I hold her for a second before she shoves free from my embrace. "Don't," is all she says before Deacon and Tyler race in behind her.

"But he—he killed you…" I stammer, unsure of what I'm seeing. The images of their dead bodies are still fresh in my mind. "I watched him kill all of you."

I push past the others and head into the living room, convinced I'll see a gory murder scene. But everything is how it was: no shattered table, no blood-splattered walls, no dead bodies.

"Did you find the pendant?" Deacon asks, but I barely hear him. My head is still reeling from what I witnessed. Mr. Shadow killed them. How are they alive?

Deacon grabs me by the shoulders. "Hey, schizo, where the hell's the necklace?"

Shaken from my stupor, I pull the triquetra from my back pocket and hold it out to them. A wave of relief washes over the group. If I didn't know better, I would've guessed none of them thought I would make it back.

Deacon pats me on the back. "Never had a doubt."

Tyler's smile fades. He glances from me and then to the kitchen. "Cody, everything's b-b-boarded up. How'd you g-g-get in?"

It wasn't real. None of it. Mr. Shadow lied to me.

I turn to the broken window and scream out at the darkness. "You liar! You said you'd kill them if I didn't make it back."

No, I told you I would make you watch.

Even though I hear him in my head, it feels like he's standing right outside the window. Why would Mr. Shadow show me that? Was it just to terrify me more or was it—

Kekoa must be thinking the same thing. "He needed a way in!" She rips the floorboard I almost impaled her with from the wall and tries to hammer it back in place. Deacon tries to grab the other pieces, but they're beyond repair. We can't cover the window.

I scan for anything we can use to block it. The heavy hand-carved kitchen table.

"Tyler, help me with this!"

Together we drag the massive table to the window. Kekoa and Deacon help, and with our combined strength we lift the huge thing onto its side and cover the window.

We can still hear the wind ripping through the opening, but there's no way Mr. Shadow is getting in without moving this table. I have no doubt he has the strength to do just that, but at least if he does, it'll make enough noise to warn us where he's coming from.

I try to tell myself that we blocked it in time, that we were only gone from this room for a second, and that if Mr. Shadow had followed me in, we'd already be dead.

I push down the nagging voice in the back of my head trying to warn me. *Just shut up and let it be.* We boarded it up in time.

"So we got the necklace," Deacon says as he leans back against the table. "What now?"

As we exchange glances, hoping someone has a plan, one thing is clear: we have no idea what we're doing. We're winging it, flying down class-five rapids on a sinking raft with no guide, no paddles, and a terrifying demon waiting just below the surface to tear us apart.

We head back to the living room, where Meadow rests next to the fire. Her head is against the wall and her eyes are closed. I have no idea how she can rest with all the pain she must be in. Those must be some seriously strong meds.

"Meadow, you didn't happen to see some giant shadow demon sneak past us in the last minute or so, did you?" Deacon asks.

Her head rolls forward and her eyes flutter open. She tries to focus on us, but her head wobbles back and forth. "I'm sorry," she slurs.

An air raid of alarm bells goes off in my head. Something is very, very wrong. She's never acted like this before. Even when she's super tired or sore, she makes an effort to at least pretend to be excited.

Tyler rushes to her side. "M-M-Meadow? Can you h-h-hear me?"

She struggles to take Tyler's hand as a tear streaks down her cheek. Her words are so slurred it's difficult to understand her. "I'm so sorry. I can't take it anymore—"

He examines both her eyes and turns to us. "They're s-s-super dilated."

"What's wrong with her?" Deacon asks.

"She's overdosing," Kekoa says as she joins Tyler at Meadow's side. "Meadow, what'd you take? You need to tell us what you took."

"I l-l-locked the m-m-meds," Tyler panics.

Tears flood down her face. "I…I can't… The nightmares…"

Then I see it. A small empty baggie in her hand. Oh, God, no…

I find my backpack on the ground, the top unzipped, and a pair of white socks next to it. No, no, no! How could she have known? My stash.

"Seroquel," I yell to the others. "She's taken all of 'em!"

"She n-n-needs to v-v-vomit," Tyler says. "Get i-i-it out of her s-s-system."

"Get outta the way." Deacon shoves Tyler aside. Tyler tries to fight, but Deacon holds him back with one hand. "Dude, I got this. I've done it enough times with my dad."

"I h-h-have to help—"

Kekoa cuts him off. "Help her by finding something in the med pack for poisonings."

Reluctantly, Tyler backs down. He goes to the med pack and digs through it.

"Roll her on her side," Deacon orders.

Kekoa and I ease Meadow over as she continues to slur her apologies. "Please forgive me… I don't deserve—"

Before she can finish, Deacon shoves two fingers down her throat. Meadow gags and convulses but doesn't throw up. He tries again, but nothing comes up.

Deacon swears as he tries a third time. "She's fighting it. Her gag reflex isn't working."

Kekoa rests Meadow's head in her lap and takes her hand. "Hey, Meadow. I need you to listen to me, okay? You gotta stop fighting us. Let us help you."

Meadow tries to turn her head away. "You don't need me…"

"Yeah, we do," Deacon argues. "This dysfunctional family would suck without you."

"I need you," I add. "You've already taught me so much about the world I see. I've been so scared of it all my life, but because of you, there's hope. There's so much you can teach me."

"I f-f-found something," Tyler says as he slides back. "Syrup of i-i-ipecac. Please, Meadow, s-s-swallow this." Tyler holds the bottle to her lips, but she pulls away.

"Just let me go…" she slurs through her crying gasps.

With a gentle touch, Kekoa runs her fingers through Meadow's green hair. "We need you, Meadow. We can't survive this without you. You've helped us every step of the way. We can't make it out of here without you."

Tyler takes her hand. "Please, Meadow. Don't leave. I love you…"

Meadow glances up at the four of us gathered around her, and for a heartbeat, I see a moment of clarity in her eyes. With a slight nod, she opens her mouth. Tyler pours the syrup of ipecac in, and after a second, she swallows.

Chapter 23

It was the longest ten minutes of my life before Meadow threw up everything in her system. Ten taut minutes of absolute fear, not knowing if we'd gotten to her in time. I thought I was watching my friend die right in front of us, and all she could say in her haze was that she was sorry. But by some miracle, she pulled through.

Deacon lowered a couch down from the barricade and set it up next to the fire. Tyler and Kekoa helped Meadow over to let her rest.

More out of habit than anything else, we decided to share our last ready-to-eat meal. No one was really hungry, but we forced down what we could. All our nerves are fried as we stare at the dark corners of the cabin, waiting for something to pop out and attack us. Nothing does, but no one is stupid enough to think we're in the clear. We sit in silence.

I keep replaying all the moments people near me have gotten hurt or worse. *I* did this. *I* brought Mr. Shadow here.

The rain finally lets up, revealing a handful of twinkling stars through the cloud cover. We're in for a long, sleepless night.

The wind slices through the cabin walls like a knife cutting my exposed skin. But I don't care. In fact, part of me welcomes it. I deserve this. I sit there and focus on the pain. It's better than what's going on in my mind.

It's Meadow who finally breaks the silence. "You guys okay?" she asks, sitting up.

Tyler rushes to her side to help her. "E-e-easy there. You gave us quite a s-s-scare."

She tries to give us a reassuring smile. "I'm fine. I promise."

"Bullshit, you're fine," Deacon snaps. "You tried to off yourself. What the hell, Meadow?"

"N-n-not now," Tyler says, but Meadow gives Tyler a gentle pat on the back of his hand.

"It's okay. I...I didn't know what else to do." She looks and sounds exhausted. "It just seemed like the better option. Better than the pain and nightmares and—"

"You c-c-could've talked to m-m-me..."

Meadow wipes a tear. "I know. I'm so sorry for putting you through this."

A wave of guilt washes over me. "What do you mean by nightmares?"

A visible chill ripples through her. "Every time I sleep, all I dream about is how much pain I've caused my family. The disappointment. How much happier they'd be without me around. Sometimes I see it when I'm awake too."

"Just reliving the highlights of the worst moments of your life." Realizing he said that out loud, Deacon adds with a sheepish glance, "I've been having some nightmares too."

"M-M-Me too."

My heart drops. I should've known Mr. Shadow would go after them. He's torturing them the same way he did my sisters. But now that he's so much more powerful, he's pushed one of us to the brink of suicide.

Kekoa sits on the outskirts of the group, double-checking the supplies. "Have you heard a voice that sounds like a metal grinder telling you to... do things?"

Meadow nods. "It told me where to find the pills." She turns to me with terror in her eyes. "It's Mr. Shadow, isn't it? He's the one doing all this."

I can't look at her; I can't look at any of them. This is all my fault...

Warm arms wrap themselves around me as something heavy and soft rests on my back. Meadow hugs me from behind. "I'm so sorry, Cody. If that's what you've been hearing your whole life, I don't know how you do it."

Nestled in her warm embrace, I want to burst into tears. It takes all my self-control not to break down in front of everyone. "Thank you," is the best I can choke out.

"Okay, okay, enough of this kumbaya shit," Deacon says. "So now we know this freaking shadow demon has been messing with all our heads. On a scale of one to ten, how screwed are we?"

"Every piece of electrical equipment is dead," Kekoa says as she clicks, reclicks, and clicks again a flashlight. "The food's gone. We've got a map and compass but no idea where we are on it. Basically we can't call anyone; we can't go anywhere on foot; and we can't stay here."

"So a twelve," Deacon sums up.

"Not necessarily," I say. "There's a path. Mr. Shadow told me it leads out of here."

Tyler shakes his head. "And you b-b-believed him?"

"He said if I took the necklace and left, I'd be free. My family would be safe."

Deacon sits up, his eyes wide and mouth agape. "You had a ticket out of here and you came back? You moron! You could've gone for help. Why the hell did you come back?"

My eyes fall on Kekoa. For a moment, her hard glare softens and the angry wrinkles in her forehead fade.

Tyler saves me. "Because we n-n-needed the p-p-pendant."

Deacon throws his hands up in frustration. "And how exactly will that help us again? Can't really use it to make a call—"

"It'll help ward off Mr. Shadow." Meadow grimaces, trying to get into a comfortable position with her splinted leg.

"Great, so we starve to death in our safe little bubble. I've got a better idea: we make a break for it. There's one of him and five of us. He can't get us all if we run in different directions."

Kekoa rolls her eyes. "So we all get lost in the woods? Alone. With that thing out there. Great plan, Einstein."

Tyler takes a protective hold of Meadow's hand. "Not e-e-everyone can run."

Deacon turns on Tyler. "Not my problem."

"Y-y-you're not helping, D-D-Deacon. Please c-c-calm—"

"Holy shit, Tic Tyler, get the marbles out of your mouth and spit it out already. Jesus Christ, after three months of therapy you'd think you'd have your shit together."

I don't know what comes over me, but I'm on my feet heading for Deacon. "Back off," I say with more courage than I'm feeling. "We're all scared, so how about you chill—"

Deacon gets in my face. "Scared? Do I look scared to you?"

"Yeah, you do."

"You need to sit down before I put you down."

I don't budge. Even though he's a head taller than me, I stand my ground. Deacon's jaw flexes and his hands clench, but before he rips off my head, Kekoa snaps. "Holy shit, will all of you just shut up?!"

Like a bull seeing the red cape of a matador, Deacon snaps right back. "I'd like to see you make me. How about you go back to sitting and moping and being completely useless or I'll—"

Kekoa just laughs at him. "Or you'll what? Beat me like your daddy beats you? Like father, like son. No-good, abusive alcoholic has to hurt others to feel good about himself. You're just as useless, if not more. And you—"

Kekoa turns her anger on Tyler. "News flash: you aren't perfect. You never will be. You'll never live up to your crazy parents' expectations, so just accept it already. The only reason you're even friends with Meadow is because she makes you feel better about yourself. At least you aren't her, right? A meek little girl pretending the world is all rainbows and butterflies because she doesn't want to face the fact that she hates herself."

"Kekoa, what are you doing?" I reach out to her, to take her hand and snap her out of whatever rage she's in, but she jerks it away.

"Don't touch me, you freak! You're the worst of all. You're a coward. You have this power, but instead of using it, you try to run from it and in the process drag all of us into your shit with you. Your family sent you away because they're better off without you. You cause pain everywhere you go. Because of you, four people are dead and we're probably next!"

I stop thinking straight and my anger boils over. "What makes you any better than us, huh? You've been in the wilderness longer than anyone here. I think it's 'cause you're too afraid to go home. You hide here in your little safety hoodie, pushing the truth down so deep because you can't deal with it. You want us to deal with our problems, fine. Let's start with yours."

Fear flashes across Kekoa's face. In a sick way, I enjoy it. She deserves it after everything she's said about the others. About me.

I turn to the group. "You guys want to know why she's here? What Mr. Shadow showed me? She's not crazy—"

Kekoa shakes her head. "Stop, Cody—"

But I don't listen. "She wasn't a drug dealer…" She reaches out for my hand, but I pull it away. "And she didn't kill anyone."

"Don't, please—"

"She was raped."

It's like I reached into her chest and ripped out her heart. She freezes, staring at me with absolute shock. No one moves. No one speaks.

"By her friend. She told her dad, but he didn't believe her. So you know what she did? She tried to kill herself. Swallowed a bunch of pills, just like Meadow. She succeeded, though. Flatlined twice in the ambulance. That's why she's here. Guess you're no better—"

I turn back to Kekoa. Her shoulders are hunched; her lower lip quivers; and a single tear glides down her cheek. She looks…broken.

As soon as I see her shattered face, I regret every word. All I've wanted to do since I got to know her was help her—and now all I've done is hurt her more than anyone else here. More than Mr. Shadow even. I reached into her most secret spot, yanked out her diary, and pulled open the pages for all to see. Noah. Being called a liar. Everything. I know the pain of isolation, of never being believed by those you love. The cold blood of regret floods my body, and all I want to do is throw myself at her feet and beg for forgiveness.

I could blame my betrayal on Mr. Shadow. Say he's feeding on our agony. It makes sense that he's using us to hurt one another. A nightmarish puppet master forcing us to say things, to cut as deep as possible to divide the group. Fan the flames of pain, terror, and hopelessness. This is what he wants so he can grow stronger. It's why he didn't show me anything from the beginning, not until Kekoa and I got close. Not until the truth would cause the most damage. He wants to tear us apart, and he waited for the perfect moment.

But Mr. Shadow isn't here. He didn't force me to say these things. All he did was plant the bomb—I detonated it. I'm the one who broke Kekoa's trust. I broke her heart.

My mind races to say something—anything—to let her know I didn't mean it, but before I can get a word out, a strange sound cuts through the silence. It's familiar, but I can't quite place it. An airy, shrill whistle echoes through the space, drawing everyone's attention.

Where have I heard that before? Then the notes change. It's not a whistle. It's music. Music we've woken up to almost every morning for the last two weeks. Marcus's harmonica.

"Do you guys hear that?" Deacon asks.

Tyler tilts his head like a deer listening for a predator. "Where's it c-c-coming from?"

A chill grips my stomach and drags it down. I know. Marcus put the harmonica in his backpack. The backpack he was wearing when he left. "It's coming from the cellar."

Meadow perks up a little. "It's Marcus."

"No, it's not," I try, but Meadow's smile doesn't falter; she's desperate for a ray of hope.

"You shut the hell up," Deacon orders. "You've screwed up enough."

"You were down there," I argue. "Marcus isn't there. He and Shawn are in the cooler."

"Did you s-s-see their b-b-bodies, Deacon?" Tyler asks.

"Couldn't see much after the lights turned off and he dragged me out," Deacon gripes.

"I'm telling you, it wasn't—"

Meadow cuts me off. "Kekoa!"

I turn to see Kekoa storm into the kitchen. "This shit ends now."

"Kekoa, no!" I take off at a full sprint with the others on my tail. Mr. Shadow must have snuck through the window right behind me before we boarded it up. This is a trap. He's leading us down into the cellar, down into the darkness.

Kekoa grabs the cellar handle. I lunge, but I'm a second too late. She pulls the door open.

The space beyond the door is pitch-black. Any light from the kitchen is sucked in and disappears. An arctic blast rushes up and nearly knocks the wind out of me.

"Come up and face us, you son of a bitch!" Kekoa screams down the stairs.

The harmonica stops. We wait in hushed anticipation, but nothing comes from below.

Another icy blast rips up the stairs, carrying a faint, grating sound. Laughter. "Kekoa, close the door," I warn, but she just stands there. We're all frozen in place, listening to the scratching laughter grow louder and louder.

Then I see him. Even in the blackness of the cellar, Mr. Shadow's silhouette is darker than everything else. The black shadow starts from the basement floor and grows like a malicious tree, taller and taller until his frame fills the doorway and his hat reaches the ceiling.

My legs are locked; my muscles are frozen; and my hands are clenched so hard I feel my nails digging into my palms. I also feel Meadow's necklace in my grip.

The triquetra! I force my arm to lift the pendant like a shield between Mr. Shadow and us.

"Leave us alone!" I scream.

But nothing happens. Mr. Shadow isn't forced back; no light flashes from the pendant; and I don't even feel an ounce of energy coming from the crystal.

Mr. Shadow laughs again, his scathing voice like a hot poker in my ear. The others hear it too, cringing away from the towering black mass and covering their ears.

Mr. Shadow's head snaps up. He's no longer a blurry shadow I'd see out of the corner of my eye. There are wrinkles in his dead skin, rot in his yellowed teeth, and cracks in his blistered lips. His sunken blue eyes stare back at me with morbid excitement.

Let's have some fun.

And the lights go out.

Chapter 24

Someone screams. For all I know it could be me. We panic. I crash into a warm body and fall to the floor. Behind me is the glow from the fireplace in the living room. I crawl on my hands and knees as fast as I can to reach that beacon of safety.

"Get to the fire!" I yell.

We scramble out of the kitchen, away from the cellar and Mr. Shadow, and into the living room. Kekoa grabs a handful of glow sticks and snaps them all at once. She throws them into the darkest corners, giving the space an eerie green glow.

There's no sign of Mr. Shadow. My heart feels like it's going to explode. He's changed. Defined, vivid. I felt his cold breath on my face.

Deacon sounds like he's about to hyperventilate. "Holyshitholyshitholyshit—what the hell was that?!"

Meadow cries into Tyler's shoulder. Tyler's lips open and close like a goldfish gasping for air. "It-it-its m-m-mouth," he tries, but can't get the words out.

Realization hits me. "Wait, you guys saw him too?"

"That's Mr. Shadow?" Meadow chokes out.

"That's what you've been seeing this whole time?" Deacon asks, stunned. "How are you even remotely sane? I'd be loaded all the time if that freaking thing was following me."

"He's different. He's changing. He's becoming—"

"Real," Kekoa finishes my thought.

I hold up Meadow's necklace. "It didn't work. He just laughed at it."

All heads turn to Meadow, who buries her face deeper into Tyler's shoulder, but even he pulls away a little. "Meadow, y-y-you said the p-p-pendant would work."

"I thought it would," she whispers.

"You *thought*?" Deacon snaps. "It was a guess? We're banking our lives on your 'expertise,' but you're just a wannabe. Just another way to seek attention."

I'm having a hard time not agreeing with him. I dove into a pool of human decay. I risked my life to go out into the woods and find that thing. All because she said it would protect us. I thought she had the answers, thought she was someone I could turn to after being alone in the dark for so long, but she's as clueless as I am.

The reality of us not getting out of here alive starts to become as tangible as Mr. Shadow. In the back of my mind, I've been hoping we could come up with a way to stop him. And when Meadow mentioned the power of the crystal, there was a glimmer of hope. There's a chance I could get back to my mom and sisters.

But now that small light has been extinguished.

Mr. Shadow is real; the others can see and hear him; and the pendant doesn't work. We're all trapped in a cabin in the middle of the woods with a murderous spectral who wants to drain us for every drop of fear we have before killing us. And there's nothing we can do to stop him.

But the last thing we need right now is to fall apart. As much as I want to blame Meadow, it's not her fault. She had an idea, and that's more than I can say for me.

"That's enough, Deacon!" I say. "Mr. Shadow's in the house and we're sitting ducks. We need a plan."

Meadow's mouth barely moves as she whispers. "I have—"

Deacon cuts her off. "Like I said, we make a break for it. Take our chances out there."

Kekoa rolls her eyes. "Another brilliant idea from the mastermind of the group."

"Shocker you take your boyfriend's side," he retorts.

"He's not my boyfriend."

I ignore her disgusted tone. "So you'd rather get lost in the woods and die of starvation."

"Better than waiting to be butchered by your freaking demon monster."

"I have an idea—" Meadow tries again.

"He's not mine!" I yell.

"This isn't C-C-Cody's fault," Tyler chimes in.

"Yeah, it is. He brought that thing here. We were doing fine before—"

"*Shut up!*" Meadow blasts.

Everyone freezes. Even Meadow is shocked by her outburst. She scans person to person hoping for a lifeline or an escape route, but there's nowhere to go. Resting her back against a wall, she lets gravity draw her down. She becomes a frightened little ball chewing on her knees. "I have an idea," she squeaks again.

Tyler puts a reassuring arm around her. It lightens the panic and stops her chewing. She turns her head to rest her cheek on her knees.

"I think I know why the crystal didn't work. It doesn't just enhance positive energy—it enhances *all* energy."

"What does that have to do with anything?" Deacon huffs.

"It worked before because we were trying to help. Cody was trying to save Kekoa, and I was trying to save Cody. But the last time, we were terrified. We were angry. That's what the crystal was harnessing."

I start to follow. "And that's what you said Mr. Shadow feeds on."

Meadow nods in agreement. "I think that's why he's changed so much, gotten so much stronger. I also think that's why he hasn't killed us."

"So if his g-g-goal was to become r-r-real, w-w-what n-n-now?"

The room falls silent. The fire crackles, causing the light to dance across the walls. The green glow stays steady but only lightens the living room. The doors and halls that lead to the rest of the cabin remain pitch-black.

Meadow takes a breath and answers, "This whole time, Mr. Shadow has been trying to isolate us, right? First the equipment, then the counselors, now this. He's trying to break us up. Make us vulnerable. Our strength is in unity."

I study the group. We're an alcoholic bully, a depressed perfectionist, a suicidal wiccan, a broken survivor, and me. We can barely hold up against our own inner demons, let alone battle a real one. I see the same thought in the others' eyes.

Meadow sees it too, but instead of letting it deter her, she doubles down. "Take Deacon for example. He can be a hot-headed douchebag sometimes—"

"Now who's being rude?" Deacon growls and crosses his arms.

"But he's fiercely protective of those he cares about. In his way, he pushes us to be better. He could've left at any time, but he's stayed. He is passionate and destructive but can also bring light and warmth. Like Fire."

Deacon's hands fall to his side as he tries to stifle a sheepish grin. He straightens his poster and flexes a little. "Yeah, sounds about right."

Meadow turns to Tyler. "Tyler, you focus on being perfect so much that you can't see the truth: you already are. You're so smart and caring, I wouldn't change a thing. You just need to believe that too. You're thoughtful, creative, and the brains of the group. You are Air."

For a moment, the fear that's on the verge of overwhelming Tyler begins to abate. A whisper of a laugh escapes, and he gives his close friend a thankful nod.

"Kekoa, you're the most stubborn, crass, intimidating person I know. You don't let anyone tell you what to do. But you're also the strongest. You carry so much—I don't know how you do it. You don't have to do it alone. You have friends. You have *us*. You can be dark and mysterious, but you're also the life-force of the group. Water."

Kekoa stands on the outskirts of the group, staring into the fire and nibbling on her thumb's cuticle. I see her gears turning, trying to figure a way out of this, but she's also using the flames as a distraction from looking at any of us, especially me. For a split second, she glances Meadow's way and pulls her hand from her mouth.

"And Cody. You're the bravest person I've ever met. If that thing has been with you for ten years, I can't imagine what your life has been like. To face that and keep going, even when you're scared, gives me the courage to overcome my struggles. Because of what you can see and your ability to overcome it, you are Spirit."

I've never been called brave before. Tough to consider when I've lived most of my life in a constant state of terror. But bravery isn't the lack of fear—it's the ability to overcome it. And I'm still here, still standing against my living nightmare. I am Spirit, which is all the more appropriate since that's what I used to call spectrals. I give Meadow a reassuring smile.

"As for me, I'm Earth. I take on the characteristics of those around me to better suit their needs. I'm a giver. But I also need to stay strong and hold to my foundations. Together, the five of us make the Pentacle. It's one of the most powerful symbols in all of human history."

Kekoa's arms are crossed. "That's great and all, but how's that going to help us?"

Meadow smiles. "We make a Devil's Trap."

Chapter 25

"This is a bad idea," Deacon repeats for the hundredth time. "A very, very bad idea."

Kekoa shrugs. "It's better than nothing."

"You're not the one going down to the cellar. Why does she get to stay up here again?"

Meadow sighs at having to repeat herself. Again. "I need her to watch my back while I make the trap." She turns her attention to me. "The salt's in the kitchen?"

I nod. "Big bag of it right next to the stove."

"And that will r-r-repel Mr. Shadow?"

Meadow hesitates. "It should create a protective barrier from evil spirits."

Deacon turns on Meadow. "What do you mean 'should'?"

"It's not like this is an exact science or…like I've ever done this before."

"And if he's not in the cellar?" I ask, trying to keep everyone focused. "What if he's somewhere else in the cabin?"

"I'll pour salt in front of each door and behind you guys after you go downstairs."

"*Should* be fun," Deacon grumbles.

"So all we have to do is get the lights working?" I confirm.

Meadow nods. "If we channel the light through the crystal and focus it on Mr. Shadow, it should destroy him."

Deacon shakes his head. "There it is again. I'm really starting to hate the word 'should.'"

"I-I-I don't th-th-think I c-c-can..." Tyler tries but can't get the words out. Meadow catches him by the hand.

"What are the main parts of a generator?" Meadow asks.

Tyler crinkles his brow in confusion but answers, "An internal c-c-combustion engine, a-a-alternator, starter, fuel tank, and outlets, b-b-but—"

"And how do they work?"

"If gas-powered, which from the description provided is what we're working with, first you run the engine. This in turn p-p-powers an onboard alternator to generate electrical power. The outlets are used for—"

Meadow smiles and squeezes his hand. "See? Already better. Focus on what you know. We need the power for the plan to work, and you're the only one who can fix the generator if Mr. Shadow did something to it. It doesn't have to be perfect. It just has to work, okay?"

Tyler takes a deep breath and nods.

"It'll work," I say with as much confidence as I can muster, but the truth is, I'm with Deacon. If anyone has something to complain about, it's me. I'm not setting

the trap, fixing the generator, or protecting the others.
We need someone to distract Mr. Shadow. I'm the bait.

It makes sense in a twisted way. If Mr. Shadow
wanted me dead, he could've killed me a long time ago.
But that was before he took on a physical form.
Now...I'm not so sure.

Each of us takes one of the five remaining glow
sticks. There was a good argument for only using three
and saving the other two, but no one wants to be the one
without light. Plus, if the plan works, we won't need
them anymore. And if it doesn't...we still won't need
them. Using the fishing line from Shawn's bag, we hang
the glow sticks around our necks.

With me in front, we head for the kitchen. In my
mind, Mr. Shadow is waiting down every hall, around
every dark corner, and behind every door. He's stalking
us, patient for the moment one of us is alone so he can
rip us into the darkness, never to be seen again.

I open the kitchen door, but as soon as the green
glow illuminates the space, I want to slam it shut. It's a
room of nightmares. Dark, thick blood drips down the
walls; the chairs and cabinets have aged a hundred years
with rot; cobwebs cover every inch; and the dining room
table centerpieces are the severed heads of Tyler,
Meadow, Deacon, and Kekoa.

I step back and bump into Tyler. "W-w-what is
it?"

"You don't see—" The kitchen is back to normal.
No blood, no rot, no severed heads. It was a
hallucination. No, a message: *This will happen if you
keep going.*

"Never mind." I point to the stove on the opposite side of the room. "The salt's over there. Make sure you put..." Kekoa clips me with a stiff shoulder check as she storms past. "...a line along the door behind us as soon as possible."

Meadow wraps her arms around Tyler, then reaches out and pulls in a surprised and uncomfortable Deacon as well. "Good luck."

Kekoa keeps her cold shoulder turned toward me. I wouldn't be able to look at myself after what I said either. An apology doesn't begin to scratch the surface, but I owe her that at least. I wouldn't even know where to begin...

Maybe making it out of this alive is a good place to start. I take hold of the cellar door. "You guys ready for this?"

"No," Deacon and Tyler say in unison.

"Me neither," I say, then open the door to the stairway to hell.

The space below is pitch-black. Deacon and Tyler stay right on my heels as I take one cautious step after another. The old wood creaks underfoot, the sound echoing in the darkness.

But as we get lower, a distant scuttling makes it through the quiet, like a centipede crawling over fallen leaves. At first, I don't really pay attention to it, but the scurrying sound grows louder with each step down. By the time we can see the floor of the cellar, the sound is no longer a single centipede but an entire army.

That's when the smell hits—it reeks like rotten eggs in a sewer. I fight every muscle in my stomach to keep the little food I have in my system down. Tyler gags.

"Oh God, what is that smell?" Deacon struggles to say between dry heaves.

As I reach the last step, I poke my head around the corner. Although the light from the glow stick doesn't reach too far into the cellar, what little I can see makes my skin crawl. The cellar is alive. The walls are thick with crickets and cockroaches; the floor is a swarm of scorpions and earthworms; and even the ceiling is covered with spiders. Every square inch of the place is moving.

Tyler joins me on the bottom step and sees the horrible sight. "Nope, nope, nope. We can't c-c-cross that."

"It's just bugs," Deacon scoffs. "Don't be such a—"

A spider the size of my hand leaps down from the ceiling and lands on Deacon's shoulder. Even in the dim light, I see the long legs covered in small hairs, all eight beady little eyes, and two massive fangs.

"Deacon, don't—"

Too late. His gaze meets the unblinking eyes, and he lets out a petrified scream. He jumps up and down, shaking violently to get the arachnid off him. The spider is launched into the darkness, but Deacon doesn't stop his dance of terror until Tyler physically grabs him.

"It's okay," Tyler tries. "It was a h-h-huntsman spider. They're not d-d-dangerous. They feed on insects and are common in Australia. But what's it doing here?"

"I don't give a shit what it's doing here," Deacon snaps, still trying to brush off other imaginary spiders. "There's no way in hell I'm crossing that. We need to go back upstairs and come up with another plan."

"There is no other plan," I protest. "This is Mr. Shadow. We have to move forward."

"So how are you getting across that?"

I have no idea. If we stay in the middle, we could avoid the walls and most of the stacked boxes, but the ground and ceiling are a different matter. The ground is crawling over itself, and nearly every inch of the ceiling is covered in spiders hanging from their webs. We'll be swarmed the second we step out there.

But why are they all waiting? Why are they stopping just short of where we are? If there are that many creepy crawlies, they could charge us like the spider did, and we'd be overrun in seconds. But they're staying back.

The pendant is in my pocket. Maybe it's working again. There's only one way to find out. I pull it out and put it on.

I take a tentative step forward. As I do, the whole floor skitters back as if an invisible field forces it away. I take another step and again the bugs retreat further.

I turn to Deacon and Tyler. "Stay close to me. They won't come near the necklace."

Deacon and Tyler huddle close as we continue forward in a giant protective bubble of glowing green light. Snakes, spiders, and bugs surround us but back off when they get too close.

"It's working," Deacon says, surprised. "Ha! Is this really the best Mr. Shadow's got?"

Before I can tell Deacon to be careful what he wishes for, we get our answer. Three screams tear over the millions of scuttling insects. At the edge of the green light, three figures hang from the ceiling. Kaylee, Haylee, and my mom are suspended in the air, impaled through the back with meat hooks, their stomachs ripped open.

"This is your fault. You did this to us!" Mom screams at me.

"You were supposed to protect us," Haylee whimpers.

"Why didn't you save us?" Kaylee cries. "You left us alone with him."

They're not real. They're not real. They're not—

"Jason!" Deacon yells. "Let my brother go, you son of a bitch!"

"M-M-Mom? Dad?" Tyler stutters, his eyes filled with terror. "I'm s-s-sorry…"

Both are staring up at my family hanging from hooks, but they're seeing their own.

"This isn't real," I snap at the other two. "It's a hallucination. Mr. Shadow's messing with our heads. They aren't here. This isn't real."

It will be. If you continue to fight the inevitable, I'll go after every soul you've ever cared about. I'll make them suffer. They'll beg me to kill them. And when they ask why I'm doing this, I'll tell them it's because of you.

"That's why we're going to stop you," I yell back.

I grab the others and force their eyes away from the grisly visions. "He's scared. That's why he's doing this. Focus on the good, don't let it leave you, and we'll make it."

Shaken but not broken, both guys nod. When I turn back, the mutilated bodies of my family have vanished. We continue. Bugs, snakes, and spiders scurry out of our way until we reach the generator and my heart plummets.

It look like it's been mauled by a grizzly bear. Twisted metal with shreds of leather hang from it with a pool of gasoline underneath. If I didn't know this was a generator before, I wouldn't know what I was looking at.

"What the hell happened?" Deacon asks.

"Mr. Shadow," is all I get out. Disappointment threatens to sap what courage I have left.

"This is i-i-impossible. I don't even know w-w-where to s-s-start. I c-c-can't—"

Deacon grabs Tyler by his collar. "I swear to God if you say you can't do this one more time, I'm going to shove this glow stick so far up your ass your head will glow like a jack-o'-lantern. If anyone can fix this hunk of junk, you can, you brainy bastard. Just look at the damn thing and tell us what's wrong."

Tyler turns back to the generator. After a few seconds, he shrugs. "It's br-r-roken."

"Listen, you sassy walking Wikipedia page, remember what Meadow told you. Don't try to make it perfect. Just make it work. What does this generator need to work?"

"Well, the l-l-lubrication system is shot and the control panel's been t-t-torn in half. The exhaust pipes are completely useless and—"

"Can you make it work?!"

Tyler examines the machine once more. "The e-e-engine and most of the electricals seem to be intact... It won't be p-p-pretty, but—"

"Good enough. So shut the hell up and get to work." Deacon turns to me. "I got his back. You help the girls finish up."

I nod to Deacon and give Tyler a reassuring hug. "You can do this."

Suddenly, all the critters start to scurry for the shadows of the cellar. There's only one thing that can make them run for their lives like this. "He's here." Dread builds in my chest. I scan the room. "Leave us alone! We're not afraid of you anymore."

You're not afraid of me anymore?

I turn. Mr. Shadow looms over Tyler and Deacon. His horrible grin spreads wide as he stares at me with his empty black eyes.

You should be.

Chapter 26

"Behind you!" I scream.

Deacon turns in time to get smashed across the face. He's lifted off his feet and launched across the cellar, sending his glow stick flying from his neck. The darkness swallows him whole.

Mr. Shadow turns on Tyler, who's frozen in fear.

I charge, but Mr. Shadow catches me by the head and easily lifts me. I try to break free, but I'm no match for his supernatural strength.

Mr. Shadow smiles.

I'm in a bit of a rush, but....I'll try to enjoy this.

He hurls me across the room, smashing me into the wooden food shelves.

I crumble to the ground. The shelves crash down on top of me, pinning me under their weight. I struggle to breathe, each intake of air gets shorter and shorter. I'm being crushed.

"P-p-please, l-l-leave me alone…" Tyler begs.

All I can do is watch Mr. Shadow reach down for Tyler's neck with his skeletal fingers. But he stops inches from his prey. Mr. Shadow's wicked smile falters. He tries to reach for Tyler, but his fingers can't get any closer.

Tyler pulls the triquetra I slipped into his pocket when I hugged him and holds the pendant out. "You c-c-can't touch m-m-me. Back off!"

Mr. Shadow laughs.

You think that pathetic stone will protect you for long?

Long enough. Deacon leaps from the shadows with a wooden chair in hand. With all his might, he swings straight at Mr. Shadow's head. But with unnatural speed and reflexes, the dark spectral catches the chair. He rips it from Deacon's grip and slams it to the ground, exploding it into a million pieces.

I'm growing tired of this game.

Mr. Shadow picks up one of the leather binding strips from the broken chair. Before Deacon can escape, Mr. Shadow wraps the leather around his throat and lifts him high off the ground.

Deacon flails, clawing at the makeshift noose as his face turns a dark blue.

I grab the shelves and lift with all my might. My muscles burn and my lungs scream. Inch by inch, the massive weight moves off me. But not fast enough. Deacon's eyes are bloodshot, his face a sickly purple, and his hands fall limply to his side.

"Let him go!" With the necklace interlaced between his fingers, Tyler cocks back a fist and swings as hard as he can. I don't know if it's thanks to the training he did with Deacon, adrenaline, skill, or just plain dumb luck, but he connects square with Mr. Shadow's jaw.

Deacon crashes to the floor. Tyler pulls the makeshift noose from his throat enough for a single breath to rush through. With that precious air, color floods back into Deacon's face. He coughs as he rips the leather free from his neck but instead of relief, his red eyes fill with fear.

"Behind—" he coughs out.

Dead-eyed, Mr. Shadow stares down at the pair. He takes hold of his dislocated jaw and snaps it back into place with a bone-chilling pop. The smile's gone, replaced by a snarl of distorted rage. Mr. Shadow unleashes a scream, exploding all the glass in the basement.

"Run, Cody!" Tyler yells.

I slide out from under the shelf and bolt for the stairs, which I take two at a time. The frigid air of Mr. Shadow's breath burns the back of my neck. If I slow down at all, even to glance back for a second, I know he'll catch me.

"Kekoa! Meadow! He's coming!" I yell up the stairs, trying to warn the girls. I pray they've finished everything. We're out of time. It's now or never.

Kekoa throws open the door. "Hurry!"

I dive through the barrier, sliding headfirst into the kitchen island. "Close it!"

Kekoa slams the door closed and bolts it shut. "Where's Deacon and Tyler? Why isn't the generator working?"

"Tyler's got the necklace. They're safe for now, trying to fix the generator. Please tell me you're done."

Meadow holds the empty bag upside down. Her eyes well up and she shakes her head.

Kekoa scans the room. "What about the salt in front of…"

I see it too. A clear break through the salt in front of the door. The scattered section leads right at me. I must have kicked it when I dove through the door.

I scramble forward on my hands and knees to push the salt back into place as something powerful crashes into the other side. A massive fissure splits the door in two. There's no way it can take another hit like that.

Kekoa slides to the ground next to me to try and fix the barrier, but we're too late.

I roll on top of her to shield her as the door explodes. Wooden stakes hurtle overhead. One cartwheels by so close to my face I smell the wood.

Mr. Shadow's dark frame fills the doorway. He stares down at the two of us, ready to tear us apart when a soft mumbling draws his attention. Meadow sits in the center of her incomplete Devil's Trap, praying.

"Whatever evil comes to me here, I cast you back; I have no fear. With the speed of wind and the dark of night, may all of your harboring take flight."

Mr. Shadow turns on Meadow.

You pathetic excuse for a human. You can't stop me. You couldn't even kill yourself. Let me show you how it's done!

He charges Meadow. But just before he can reach her, Meadow drops the salt she had in her hand and completes the small circle around her. The invisible barrier around Meadow stops Mr. Shadow's hand.

Meadow continues to pray. "With the swiftness of the sea and all the power found in me, as I will, so mote it be."

This only enrages Mr. Shadow further. He punches and claws at her, but each strike stops short. The house vibrates with each powerful blow, and the salt barrier shakes with each hit. The circle won't hold for long.

"Cody," Kekoa struggles. A piece of the shattered door is impaled in her shoulder. "We need to get to the living room."

"Come on. I got you." I pull her good arm around my shoulder and help her to her feet.

We stumble toward the living room when Meadow calls out to us. "Get out now!"

No one leaves!

Mr. Shadow turns from Meadow and charges after us.

We race across the living room, nearly tripping over the large floral rug, and head for the front door. The light from the fireplace and my glow stick illuminates the area enough to see where we're going. Then, feet from the door, we stop dead in our tracks.

Wearing a sky-blue muumuu adorned in white hibiscus flowers, a tall woman with long raven hair and electric-blue eyes stands poised before the door. I can see the family resemblance.

Kekoa goes limp in my arms. "Mom?"

"Key, you're hurt." She reaches for her daughter. "Come here. Let me hold you."

Kekoa takes a tentative step toward her. "Why are you here?"

I grab Kekoa by the hand. "That's not your mom! Don't listen to—"

"I've missed you so much, my little Key."

Kekoa lets go of my hand and walks toward the woman. "I've missed you too."

Let her go, Cody. Mr. Shadow whispers behind me.

I snap around to see him standing in the hallway with the sinister smile back.

It's over.

"No," I try, but my strength is fading.

Your plan failed. The generator is destroyed. The trap is incomplete. All is lost. Give up. Stop fighting the inevitable.

Kekoa wraps her arms around her mother in a warm embrace. "Why'd you leave, Mom?"

"Oh, my little Key. I left because of you."

Kekoa looks like her mom just stabbed her in the heart. "What? Don't say that."

"She's not real, Kekoa! It's Mr. Shadow. He's using your pain," I yell, but Kekoa can't tear her eyes away from the woman she hasn't seen since she was a child.

It's real enough to her.

Kekoa's mother pulls away from the embrace. "You were such a little shit. Always begging for my attention. '*Mommy*' this and '*Mommy*' that—you drove me insane. Always such a disappointment. I needed to get away from you."

Kekoa falls to her knees. "Mom, stop. Please."

Mr. Shadow stalks toward us, stepping onto the floral rug, and turns to me.

This will all be over soon. Then I'll take you away from here. We have such a bright future ahead of us. So much delicious potential. We must be ready for what's to come.

Kekoa cries at her mother's feet. "I'm so sorry, Mom."

"You can't do anything right. You couldn't even kill yourself," Kekoa's mom spits.

"Kekoa, don't listen!"

You can't protect her. You can't protect anyone. It's all going to end. It'll be biblical. This is a mercy in comparison.

"You won't touch anyone!" I yell, backing up until I'm standing next to Kekoa.

"Stop fighting, Key. Do something right for the first time in your life. Do the world a favor and just end it already."

"You're right, Mom. This needs to end." Kekoa's cheeks are streaked with tears. "Cody…we good?"

I nod. "Yeah. We're good."

Mr. Shadow reaches out for me with his impossibly long, skeletal fingers, but they stop short. Confusion crosses his face. He tries harder to grab me, his smile turning to a grimace of strain and frustration, but he can't get any closer. His fingers slam into an invisible barrier again and again.

This is impossible. The pendant is in the cellar. How are you–

Kekoa reaches for the floral rug and lifts a corner. Underneath is a thick line of salt between Mr. Shadow and me. As she wipes her tears, a wicked smile of her own crosses her face. "Got you, you bastard."

Chapter 27

Meadow peeks her head into the living room. "Did it work?"

Mr. Shadow charges Meadow. She jumps and lets out a little squeak, but before he can reach her, the dark spectral crashes into an invisible wall. He roars in frustration, but it's muted like he's in a giant fish bowl.

Meadow makes her way into the living room, careful not to take her eyes off the demon staring daggers at her.

"You sure that shit'll hold up?" Deacon comes around the corner, leaning heavily on Tyler. Meadow hobbles over to the two guys and wraps her arms around them in a tight hug. Deacon groans. "Easy there, turbo."

"Meadow, you're a genius," Tyler beams.

"Did you get the generator to work?"

Tyler nods and tosses me the crystal pendant. "It's not p-p-pretty, but it'll do."

Let me out of here!

Mr. Shadow slams his bony fists against the invisible barrier again and again. The walls of the cabin shake with each massive blow, but the barrier doesn't break.

I will rip you apart. I will feast on your souls. I will make you suffer—

"All the more reason to get rid of you," I say. "Let's do this."

The five of us circle Mr. Shadow as he stalks back and forth like a caged tiger. We each grab a section of the rug and fold it in, revealing a salt star with intricate circles at the five points. We stand at our designated spots: Water for Kekoa, Fire for Deacon, air for Tyler, Earth for Meadow, and Spirit at the top for me.

Why?

I stand on my mark right next to an old wooden standing lamp. "We're not afraid of you. I'm not afraid of you."

You think it's me you should be afraid of? We've had a good thing going for so long. Have you asked yourself why? Why would I change? Why now?

I try to block out his words. Mr. Shadow's trying to get into my head. He's trying to save himself. He knows we have him beat.

The last part of the plan is on me. I hold up the pendant in front of the lamp. "It doesn't matter. This is goodnight for you." I flip the light switch.

A brilliant fluorescent light floods the room. A beam of concentrated light energy erupts from the pendant. Mr. Shadow shrinks back and screams in agony as the beam strikes him.

Meadow brings her hands together under her chin and prays under her breath.

Deacon laughs. "Die, you bastard!"

I shine the beam of light right into Mr. Shadow as he curls into a ball in the center of the salt star. This is it. It's finally over. After years of torment, it's done. No more nightmares for the twins. No more dark shadows in the corner, no more fear. We've beaten him.

Suddenly his cries of pain change into cackles. His cackles then turn into cabin-shaking laughter. Mr. Shadow rises from his fetal position and faces me with his head at a disjointed angle, showcasing his decayed smile and sunken eyes.

I'm not done with you yet.

He opens his mouth. Like the dislocated jaw of a python, the gaping maw stretches down until it's long enough to swallow my head whole. Inside is nothing but darkness. Hundreds of screams blast from the void, a cacophony of pain and fear. The cabin rumbles from the force. The lamp falls and the light bulb shatters, hurling us back into the darkness. Although I cover my ears, my hands can't stop the deafening hell screech.

The salt at my feet shifts. The spirit design disappears like an Etch A Sketch drawing. "Protect the circle!" I yell to the others.

They all see the same thing. The awful truth dawns on us all: if the circle breaks, Mr. Shadow will be free, and we'll have no chance against him.

You can't control me!

I dive to the ground, pushing and pulling the grains of salt to keep the circle intact, but it's a losing battle. The cabin is shaking too violently for us to maintain the circle.

You can't stop me!

Windows explode and glass rains down. Blood pours from my hands as I sweep glass and salt back into place. The salt seeps into my open wounds and burns, but I don't stop. I can't—we have to hold him back.

I am pain incarnate!

The others struggle to maintain their parts of the circle. Then I see it: a thin stretch of the circle just outside Meadow's reach. Only a few grains of salt remain connected. And there's nothing I can do.

A final raging blow shakes the foundation of the cabin, and the last remaining grains of salt shift apart. The fragile connection is broken.

Mr. Shadow's piercing laugh echoes through the living room.

My turn.

A powerful shock wave erupts from Mr. Shadow, launching the others back. They're sent flying across the living room and crashing hard into the cabin walls. Meadow cries out in pain as the makeshift splint shatters. A pool of blood grows beneath Deacon's still body. Tyler tries to crawl to Meadow, but one of his arms lies useless at his side. Blood seeps between Kekoa's fingers as she tries to apply pressure to her bleeding shoulder.

When the shock wave hits me, it's like a torrent of water splitting around a boulder. The invisible force crashes into my chest but doesn't lift me off my feet. I stand against it.

How am I... Then I see the crystal pendant in my hand. I feel energy pour from it and realize it's mine. The pendant is harnessing my energy and protecting me with it. Not my anxiety or my fear but my resilience. My courage.

Mr. Shadow sees me standing in defiance and channels all his rage in my direction. Wave after wave of malicious energy slams against me, but I stand strong. I won't back down. I won't let him hurt anyone anymore.

You are pitiful. Your courage will fail. You will give in to your pain, and when you've lost all hope, I will win. You can't fight what's coming!

I feel the strain the pendant is under. It shakes in my hand so hard I have to squeeze it to keep it from shattering. The pendant won't last much longer.

My body is also about to fail. A boulder of immense pressure sits on my chest as wave after wave of drowning energy washes over me. My muscles won't stop shaking. My knees buckle and my vision starts to close in. All I can focus on is Mr. Shadow's horrifying mouth. Those rows of jagged, rotten teeth that want to tear into my flesh and rip me apart. Beyond, complete emptiness closes in on me.

But there's a glimmer of light. A distant twinkling star in the emptiness of space. I reach for it, drawing what little energy I can to urge it forward. As the beacon grows, I hear my family. Mom, Haylee, and Kaylee are giggling, the kind of carefree laughter we'd share in the fall when we'd play in piles of leaves.

There are other voices too. I gaze into the light and see my friends. Tyler, Meadow, Deacon, and Kekoa—they're all happy and healthy.

I pull back from the darkness. Mr. Shadow looms over me, the pendant ready to shatter, and my fist tightens around it.

He bites down as I swing my fist with the clenched pendant. I connect with his jagged teeth and they shatter like glass. My arm disappears into the darkness up to my elbow, and Mr. Shadow's eyes fly open in shock.

He chokes and coughs, wrapping his bony fingers around my arm and face, trying to force me away, but I keep pushing forward. It feels like I've plunged my arm into the Arctic Sea, and it goes numb. But I can't stop. I *won't* stop.

The distant star inside the darkness grows brighter and brighter. Blinding light shoots from Mr. Shadow's eyes and mouth, filling the room with a warm, enchanting aura. A million pins and needles stab my arm buried down Mr. Shadow's throat, and I once again feel the pendant in my tight grip.

The entire cabin quakes again. Mr. Shadow shakes as more and more light bursts from him. Out of his arms, his back, even his chest, radiant light erupts from his darkness.

With a final burst of brilliant energy, Mr. Shadow explodes. The remaining windows blow out as the shock wave shakes the cabin's foundation. I shield my eyes as his darkness disintegrates in the eruption of blinding light.

I collapse, drained to within an inch of unconsciousness, the pendant still vibrating with intense energy. What the hell was that? I close my eyes. Just for a second. Just for—

Something smacks my face. "Ow," is the best I can mumble. "What's that for?"

Kekoa crawls over and rests her head on my chest. "You need to stay awake. You could have a concussion."

A flood of joy washes over me and I laugh—a deep, wonderful laugh I haven't felt in forever. My ribs throb with each breath, but I don't care. I just feel…happy.

It's over. Mr. Shadow's gone.

Meadow uses Tyler as a crutch as the two hobble over. Tyler lowers her onto the couch. Deacon is right behind them, using his shirt to stem the flow of blood from a deep laceration on his bicep. He flops into a nearby La-Z-Boy.

Meadow examines the scorch mark on the rug where Mr. Shadow was standing. "So did we win?"

All four friends turn to me with expectant eyes. It takes me a second to remember I'm the only one who can see spectrals. I nod. "Yeah, we won."

"Hell, yeah!" Deacon cheers, then grabs his rib cage. He looks at each of us and shakes his head. "No joke, we look like shit."

He isn't wrong. Bruised, bloodied, and broken, we just survived a war. But we beat the darkness that's been haunting me for years. We defeated Mr. Shadow.

We lay there together, and for the first time in I don't know how long, I hear a bird chirp. I turn my head and gaze out the shattered window. A sparrow sits on a nearby branch, its elegant song echoing in the morning silence. The sun peeks above the treetops, casting a warm glow through the boarded windows. It's a new day.

Kekoa rolls onto her side and stares at me with her gorgeous green eyes and warm smile. She takes a deep breath. "So what now?"

I don't know and I don't care. Mr. Shadow is gone, I have my friends, and I'm happy. At this moment, that's all I need.

Chapter 28

Warm sunlight breaks through the vertical blinds of the hospital room and shines down on my face, waking me from my peaceful slumber. As I stretch out, careful not to pull on the wires and tubes attached to me, I feel a small pop in my lower back. I relax back into the soft bed and glance to the closet on the opposite side of the white room. The door is wide-open with enough ambient light for me to see inside. Just some clothes my mom brought from home for me to change into when they finally release me. No cold, no darkness, no Mr. Shadow.

There are still nights I wake up in a cold sweat, his shadow hiding in the outskirts of my vision, his voice grating in my ear. I can't shake what he said, always repeating the same things:

You think it's me you should be afraid of?

Why would I change? Why now?

You can't fight what's coming!

As I play them over and over in my head, there's one thing I keep hearing in his voice: fear. Mr. Shadow was afraid. At first, I thought it was us. I thought he was afraid of dying. But the more I think about it, the less I'm sure...

A knock at my door interrupts my train of thought. Two small, stacked heads press their noses against the glass. My sisters wave when they see me and I signal them to come in.

The door flies open and Haylee and Kaylee charge in. "Today's the day! Today's the day!" they chant, hopping on the bed and smothering me in hugs.

Mom comes in right after them, a huge smile on her face.

"I get to go home today?"

"You all do."

The "New Beginnings Survivors," as the news reports have christened us, have been locked away in St. Luke's Boise Medical Center for more than a week now. Segregated from the others, I've been poked, prodded, bled, scanned, scrubbed, swabbed, questioned, psychoanalyzed, and interviewed nearly every waking moment since we were flown in via helicopter.

Honestly I don't remember much after we defeated Mr. Shadow. I had never felt so drained in my life. At some point, Tyler grabbed one of the dead SAT phones and jimmied something together that charged it up enough to get a call out. A helicopter flew in and airlifted us out. They hooked me up to an IV and then I was out. The next thing I remember is waking up in my hospital room, with a million doctors, nurses, police, and reporters all trying to talk to me at the same time. That's when I heard Mom's voice explode over the crowd.

She used some colorful language I didn't know she possessed and kicked them all out. Haylee and Kaylee were there, trying to hold back tears. As soon as the last nurse left, the floodgates opened for all of us. We just hugged and cried together. They told me the others were all okay and in their rooms across the hall.

I didn't get to see my friends at all over the last week. The police kept us separated because of the investigation. A few of them thought we had somehow colluded in the murders of our counselors. They did let Dr. Hane drop in a few times. She eventually told the cops to back off, saying we were "too traumatized to remember the actual events and created an imaginary monster to cope."

The news was my only source of information. I wasn't surprised when it was reported that the police had nothing to go on. Tough to find evidence to indict a ten-foot-tall dark spectral. The suspect list was always interesting though. There were the typical guesses: the five of us, crazed mountain lions or bears, a terrorist attack, or some disturbed alumni. But there were the more eccentric ones as well, like psycho-inbred locals, a new devil-worshiping cult, and even a man-eating Bigfoot. That last one was my favorite, especially when "experts" came on the news to explain how the evidence proved it.

But the day has finally arrived—the day I get to go home. Part of me is a little apprehensive. I don't know what my life is going to be like without Mr. Shadow there. Will it be different? What if nothing changes? Can I handle going back to a life I thought was awful because of Mr. Shadow, only to find that it's that way because of me?

But the rest of me is good to go. Now I know I have the strength to face anything that stands in front of me. Bullies, grades, girls, acne—all the problems a typical teenager faces pale in comparison to what I went through. If I can survive being stuck in the woods with Mr. Shadow, I can handle high school.

Mom is in a chair next to me while Haylee and Kaylee lie in my arms when a nurse pushing a wheelchair comes in. "You ready?" she says, smiling.

I squeeze my little sisters once more. "Let's get out of here."

After a few minutes of being detached from the monitors and drips, and changing into my normal clothes, I'm plopped into a wheelchair and rolled out.

We turn the corner to the lobby where the others are with their families. Deacon still has a neat row of stitches in his arm; Tyler's black eye has turned a deep purple; Meadow's still in a wheelchair with a thick neon-green cast on her leg; and Kekoa has her arm in a sling, but they're all smiling and laughing.

Meadow is the first to see me roll up. "Cody!"

Deacon smiles and adds. "Better late than never."

Before the nurse can stop the wheelchair, I'm up and running over to the others. We all hug, but gingerly.

"You okay?" Tyler asks.

"Yeah, I'm fine."

"Lucky we're not all in jail after the freaking cops gave us the third degree," Deacon grumbles. "Treating us like we're suspects."

"We *are* treatment kids. Not to mention the last ones to see the counselors alive," Tyler points out. "Wouldn't be good at their jobs if they didn't suspect us."

"None of that matters now," Meadow says. "It's over. Finally we get to go home."

"It *is* over, right?" Kekoa asks with a shadow of concern. "You don't, you know, see anything?"

I scan the foyer. It must be a rather slow day at the hospital. Our families are off by the front door talking to one another; two nurses walk by with a stack of manila folders; and a handful of patients sit in the waiting area, but besides that, the room is pretty empty.

The spectrals are a different story. With all the emotions and energies hospitals contain, they must be a homing beacon for both light and dark creatures. Most are no bigger than the palm of my hand. Tiny light-colored geckos with wings flutter overhead and hang from the ceiling; a few dark cockroaches scurry underneath the tables and gurneys; and even a glowing cat-chinchilla hybrid is curled up on the front desk. The room is alive with all sorts of energies.

"It's all good." I smile. "How are you guys holding up?"

"We'll survive," Kekoa answers. "I think we know none of us are cured or anything like that, but we're moving in the right direction, and that's what counts."

"Steve, Jeremy, Marcus, Shawn—they gave their lives to help us," Meadow adds. "The least we can do is be better for them."

"They'd want us to get better for ourselves," I counter. "But that doesn't mean we can't be there for one another."

"Yeah, so if any of you delinquents, you know, need me to beat up a bully or something, you've got my number," Deacon offers.

"Will do," Tyler says, reaching out a hand to him. "Thank you for being there and protecting me. I don't know what would have happened—"

Before Tyler can finish, Deacon wraps him in a strong embrace. So no one gets the wrong idea, he gives Tyler a quick noogie before breaking away. "I'll catch you losers later!" he calls out as he walks to his mom and little brother.

"I have to get going too. Flight's leaving soon." Meadow sniffles. "I'll miss you guys so much. Please stay in touch, okay?"

"Of course," Kekoa says. "You're our hero after all."

"Seriously," I say as Meadow blushes. "We wouldn't be here if it weren't for you. Thank you for saving our lives."

"Me? You're the one who blew up Mr. Shadow." Meadow laughs.

"Come on. I'll roll you out." Tyler hugs Kekoa and me before grabbing the back of her wheelchair. "I love you guys."

Kekoa and I wave goodbye as the two join their families and head out the doors.

A tornado of butterflies swirls in the pit of my stomach, and my heart threatens to erupt from my chest with each pounding pulse. I've thought about this moment every second of every day since we were rescued. Me and Kekoa alone. Since we were separated and locked away, I never got the chance to apologize. But now, as I stand here next to her, everything I've planned to say vanishes from my brain. Like a wave washing over a footprint in the sand, her emerald eyes wipe my mind clean.

But I need to say something. With a shaky breath, I start. "So I wanted to talk about—"

Kekoa starts at the same moment. "I think we need to talk—"

"I didn't mean to interrupt—"

"My bad, you were saying—"

We stop talking over each other at the same time, long enough to share an anxious giggle. Kekoa digs a nervous thumb into the palm of her other hand. "This isn't easy for me, so if you don't mind, I'd like to start."

That's never good. Here comes the 'I never want to see you again' speech. Might as well rip off the Band-Aid. "Go for it."

Kekoa takes a deep breath. "Back at the cabin, after Meadow almost… I was so angry and scared. I didn't know what to do. Everyone was fighting and I couldn't take it anymore. I snapped. I wanted to hurt something. Especially you. I think because you remind me of someone I have unresolved anger issues with. But that's not an excuse for the things I said. You aren't a freak or a coward. You laid your life on the line to protect us. You gave us hope. You're the bravest person I know. Cody, I'm so sorry."

A tidal wave of relief washes over me. She doesn't want to ban me from her existence. She wanted to apologize. With the anchor of dreaded anticipation cut free, my apology pours out. "No, *I'm* sorry. It doesn't matter what you said—I never should've tried to hurt you back. Especially with that. It wasn't my truth to tell. I took away your chance to tell the others in your own time. I'm so sorry for betraying your trust like that."

"Yeah, that sucked," Kekoa agrees. "But to be honest, once I got past being pissed at you—and I was *pissed*—I realized I felt relieved. I was glad the others finally knew. After keeping it from everyone for so long, it was like a weight had been lifted. Maybe that means I'm ready to talk about what happened. All of it."

A genuine smile crosses my face. "I'm happy to hear that."

For all the anticipated outcomes of this conversation I played out in my head over the last week, this wasn't one of them. As I stand next to Kekoa, my smile shifts to an awkward grin. Where do we go from here?

"You coming or what?" Haylee calls out to me from the foyer doors.

I guess I'm going home with my family, but what about Kekoa? I don't think her dad's going to make the flight to come pick her up. I try to break the awkward moment, the words coming out before I can think them all the way through. "Do you need a place to stay?"

The instant blush on her cheeks and dimples in her smile launch my soul from my body with burning-hot embarrassment. There aren't enough nurses or doctors here to drag it back in. I'd rather die.

"Actually I got one," Kekoa smiles.

"Where—" but before I can even get the question out, a tall woman with long flowing black hair sprinkled with streaks of gray steps into the lobby. "Wait, that's—"

"My mom," Kekoa beams. "She came as soon as they released our names. We've spent the last week catching up on a lot. Turns out my piece-of-shit father has been keeping all the letters she's been writing me. He didn't even bother showing up, so I'm going to be staying with her for a while. You want to meet her?"

Before I can respond, Kekoa waves her mom over. Even though her mother is a decade older than what I saw in the cabin, Kekoa is the spitting image of her. Not just with their hair and athletic build, but even their confident walk and aura. Kekoa's mom is both casual and strong, with a pair of dark aviators on top of her head, holding back her long flowing raven hair; a tan leather jacket accentuating her broad shoulders; and form-fitting jeans over a pair of well-worn combat boots. Her only jewelry is a woven string necklace with a hand-carved wooden triangle with serrated edges hanging from the bottom that bears a rough resemblance to a shark tooth. Kekoa called her a "beautiful badass." Now it makes sense.

As she gets closer, I can't help notice her crystal-blue eyes. Eyes just like mine.

Then something saunters out from behind her that makes the air catch in my throat. I stare at the light spectral with shock, awe, and a bit of fear. I've never seen anything so majestic and powerful. At first glance, it looks like a panther. Its long sleek build flows with energy, crackling with each powerful step. Its beautiful cat eyes scan the other spectrals, all of which have stopped to stare at it. Instead of a mouth, this spectral has an eagle's beak. And fur. No, not fur—feathers. Rippling like a field of golden wheat in a gentle breeze.

Kekoa's mom smiles and shakes my hand. "Hey there. I'm Lani Makanani. You must be Cody. My daughter has told me a lot about you."

Lani winks at Kekoa, who glares back at her, but I swear she's blushing too.

I try to respond but have a hard time taking my eyes off the large wingless griffin spectral preening its feathers.

Lani sees me staring and smiles. "She's breathtaking, isn't she?"

"Mom!"

"I'm not talking about you." Lani turns back to me. "This is Hoku, my familiar."

At the mention of her name, the large spectral's ears perk up and it strides over to Lani's side. Within petting distance, I have to force my hand from reaching out.

"Is that a *uhane*?" Kekoa asks. I can only imagine how strange her mother and I look, staring at what would be empty space.

Hoku looks me right in the eyes. There's no fear, no worry, just a powerful sense of tranquility. Then, before I can move, Hoku steps away from Lani and brushes against my hip.

A static charge of electricity courses through my leg. I feel the energy from Hoku jolt through my body. The only sensation I can compare it to is the feeling of pure excitement on Christmas morning seeing presents under the tree. Joy, excitement, love, happiness—all in one burst of energy.

"She likes you," Lani says with a hint of surprise.

"And for those of us who can't see what's going on?" Kekoa interjects.

"Sorry," I say, pulling my eyes away from the spectral. Hoku returns to Lani's side to continue preening. "What's going…? How can you…? A familiar? I have so many questions."

Lani smiles at my inarticulate stumbling. "I'm sure you do. To answer one: a familiar is a spectral partner for clairvoyants. Those of us with the vision. Like you. Hoku and I have been together for a long time. Longer than you and your previous…companion."

I stare back slack-jawed and wide-eyed. Lani's smile grows wider. "I'm a clairvoyant?"

"There's so much for you to see, Cody. So much to learn." She scratches Hoku behind her ear. "It's a magical world full of mystery and wonder, made of beautiful dreams and terrifying nightmares. If you'd like to see all it has to offer, to experience its breathtaking splendor, reach out to me. It's the least I can do since you saved my daughter."

"Yeah, I'd like that," I croak out.

"Wonderful." Lani reaches into her pocket and pulls out a homemade bracelet of onyx black cordage with white pearls. "Before I go, I'd like you to wear this."

I take the bracelet from her and put it on. The pearls are cool against my skin.

"It's a little something a colleague of mine put together. This should help keep that aura of yours hidden from most dark spectrals. Don't want a repeat of—"

"Mom…" Kekoa warns.

Lani stifles a smirk. "Well, it was a pleasure meeting you, Cody. I'll leave you two to it."

As she turns to leave, she leans to Kekoa and whispers, "He's a cutie."

Kekoa turns sunset red and purses her lips. "Bye, Mom!"

I try my best to hide it, but my face is on fire. "So, uh, that's your mom? She seems nice."

Kekoa lets out an exasperated sigh. "Not the subtlest person you'll ever meet."

"I was wondering where you got that from."

She punches me in the shoulder. "Oh, shut up. We've got some stuff to work through, but we have time. I'm just happy she's here. Listen, since I'll be on the mainland now, don't be a stranger, okay?"

"Yeah, okay," I blurt out as the heat in my face rises and my heartbeat roars in my ears. Kekoa stands there, staring at me with those intense green eyes, and I find an interesting crack in the floor. "So I guess I gotta get going."

"Oh, uh, yeah. Okay," she mumbles. "I guess I'll see you around."

"For sure." I want to slap myself. Do something! I beg, but my body has forgotten how to function. Instead, as I stand there, Kekoa starts to follow her mom. She glances over her shoulder and gives me a quick wave. I give a feeble one back.

I turn and see my family waiting for me by the front door. I absolutely, completely, and utterly blew that. I'm a sorry excuse for a human being. I had it—the perfect moment to tell her how I feel—but I just stood there. I can face my demon, but when I try to tell Kekoa the truth, I freeze.

As I kick myself with each step, a soft hand turns me around. Without a word, Kekoa pulls me close and kisses me. It's the longest, happiest, most exhilarating second of my life. Then, just as fast as it happens, it stops.

Kekoa pulls back, beaming. "Call me." She turns and runs down the hall to catch up to her mom. Lani waves goodbye to me again, and they disappear down the hallway.

My heart feels like it's going to burst from my chest and dance around the hospital foyer. My cheeks hurt from smiling so hard. I turn and see my family staring at me.

"Oh, my God, that is soooo gross," Kaylee yells, then starts gagging.

Haylee makes kissing sounds and sings, *"Cody and Kekoa, sitting in a tree…"*

"Leave him alone, you two." My mom tries but fails to hide the huge smile on her face.

I don't care. Kaylee keeps pretending to throw up, and Haylee sings her song on repeat, but at this moment, although I'm a little embarrassed that it happened in front of my family, everything is perfect. I could take on a hundred Mr. Shadows and not even break a sweat. For the first time since I can remember, I feel pure, absolute, complete happiness.

When I step outside and feel the sunlight on my face, it takes a moment for the world to come into focus. I shield my eyes, and when they adjust, I'm amazed. The world before me is vibrant and alive with spectrals of all shapes and sizes. It really is a world full of mystery and wonder—and I can't wait to see it all.

Acknowledgments

Wilderness was born from my time teaching at a dual-diagnosis residential adolescent treatment center—a place often misunderstood, like the teens it served. I arrived carrying the same assumptions many do: that these were "bad kids." I couldn't have been more wrong. They were some of the most remarkable, resilient young people I've ever met. Misrepresented, underestimated, and deeply human, they inspired me to write a story where anyone—especially those who feel overlooked— could be the hero of their own journey.

To every student who walked through my classroom door: thank you. Your courage, humor, and honesty left a mark on me, and your stories live in these pages more than you know.

To Morgan, Sarah, Nathan, Robert, and all my incredible beta readers: your passion, curiosity, and feedback helped turn this dream into something real.

To my family: thank you for a lifetime of support, for reading every strange story I ever scribbled, and for always encouraging me to grow.

And to Carissa, my partner: thank you for embracing every half-formed idea with excitement, for being my sounding board, anchor, and teammate. You gave me the space to be brave and the courage to let go. This story made it into the world because you believed it should.

About the Author

Hunter Swanson's debut novel, *Wilderness*, is the first in a planned five-book series. The story was inspired by two defining experiences: years spent studying story and years spent living it—particularly as a teacher at a dual-diagnosis residential adolescent treatment center. The strength, vulnerability, and humanity of the students there became the heart of this book.

Hunter holds a BA in Literature, an MA in English, and an MFA in Screenwriting, where he graduated as valedictorian. His work has earned recognition in international competitions and won multiple awards in the horror and thriller genres. For the past eight years, he has also built a career as a creative copywriter, telling stories professionally in a different arena.

When he's not writing fiction, Hunter can usually be found rewatching classic horror films, playing Dungeons & Dragons with friends and family, wandering with a notebook and fishing pole, or dreaming up new ways to terrify readers—while still making them feel seen.

To learn more, please visit: hunterswansonbooks.com.

Excerpt from Tundra

Before I hop off my perch to return to my family, I notice the Christmas lights at the distant campsite flicker and fade, leaving just the bonfire's glow to stave off complete darkness. A shadowy wave sweeps across the campgrounds, engulfing every source of light in its path. One by one, the lampposts blink out. The air, once filled with the twang of country music, now hums with a chorus of confused groans and slurred complaints. The thickening darkness advances toward us. Maybe they killed the power for the meteor shower?

The ambient temperature plummets, sending a chill through my bones. Temperatures drop at night in the desert, but this is different. An alarm blares in my mind, a sense of dread that is all too recognizable. Something is here. I need to get my family out of here, but I can't freak them out. If I come charging in panicking about an impending darkness, Mom will think I'm having an episode and try to talk me through it, but then it'll be too late. I have a minute, maybe less, before the darkness reaches us.

Mom is instructing my sisters on the perfect golden marshmallow when she spots me. "You okay, sweetie? You look like you've seen a..." She catches herself.

She's not far off, so I run with it. "To be honest, I'm not feeling good. Probably something I ate. I don't think I'm going to make it. I really appreciate what you're trying to do, but I think we should call it. This was a great first step, but it's time to head home."

The twins snap around in their chairs. "What about our wishes?"

"You'll be able to make all the wishes you want in the car," I answer.

But Mom won't give up that easily. "Dr. Hane warned us it was going to be tough. It is for me too. It's my first time camping since... Maybe your stomach ache is in your head?"

She's wasting time. "I don't want to do this anymore. We can camp in the backyard or something. I'm not ready for this, okay? Please, let's go home."

Three beams of light cut through the darkness near the boulders, revealing the father and son from the motorhome as well as a wire-thin woman dressed in a puffy camo vest over an orange wool hoodie and weathered jeans tucked into worn combat boots. With her mess of curly brown hair in a high bun, she's almost as tall as her son.

She greets us with a wave. "Howdy, neighbors. Sorry to intrude. We just lost our power. Seems like it's going out everywhere. We didn't get a fire going," she gives a sharp look to her husband, "so can we warm ourselves here a sec? We'll be out of your hair in a jiffy. Promise."

Mom flashes her trained bank teller smile. "Of course. If you want, you're more than welcome to grab some of the coals and—"

"Best keep to the light," the rotund man interrupts, warming his hands near the fire. "Wards off any dangerous animals. You know, mountain lions and the like. Never know what's hunting out there in the dark."

The woman catches him with an elbow to the ribs. "Don't mind Mark, he's just a grumpy old fart who's forgotten his manners. I'm Judith by the way and this is our son, Logan."

"Stepson," Mark clarifies.

The tall teen hangs back, more interested in the sky than pleasantries.

Mom puts a protective arm around the girls. "You're welcome to whatever you need to get your fire started, but this is a special evening with my kids and I'd like to keep it that way."

A series of harsh chirps and whistles chime from the spectral above. I've never heard a spectral like that before. Most sound melodic or serene. This one, however, seems a warning.

"She's right," Logan says, turning from the sky. "Let's leave them alone and—"

The halogen light above our tent blinks out, plunging us into near darkness. The dying glow of our fire casts long shadows that dance across the ground.

Goosebumps prickle along my forearms and an icy tremor races up my spine, settling at the base of my skull.

"Looks like it's time for the meteor shower," Mom says with a conversation-ending shrug. "If you don't mind taking what you need and heading back, we'd really appreciate it."

But Judith and Mark aren't listening. Both shine their flashlights into the dark desert. Judith turns to me, her polite facade replaced with an intense stare. "Cody, get your family outta here. Now." Before I can even process how she knows my name, Judith grabs my mom's elbow and starts dragging her to the car. Haylee and Kaylee stay latched to Mom's side, unnerved by the sudden shift in the stranger's demeanor. Mom struggles against her grip, but Judith holds fast.

A twig snaps behind us. The drunk college guy in a pink sweater stumbles out of the darkness. A dark splash soaks his right collarbone and drips down the front of the Greek letters. His movements are erratic, like the signals to his muscles are short circuiting. He opens his mouth to speak, but black ichor pours out. The scent of sweet metal permeates my brain. Blood. Struggling to move his arms, his panicked eyes plead for help.

A guttural hiss threatens from the shadows. Eight large jaundice orbs and a pair of katana-sized jagged obsidian pincers manifest from the darkness. A flowing mane of dark static electricity encircles a short muzzle filled with long teeth and two hooked mandibles. Four powerful legs end in thick paws with five-inch claws digging into the sand. A thick segmented tail wraps over its massive frame and ends in a curved black sickle. The dark spectral is a nightmarish amalgamation of lion and scorpion.

In a blur of dark spectral energy, the large stinger pierces the man's back.

Dark veins snake up his neck and spread across his face, their necrotic hue marking the path of the venom. His eyes become pools of obsidian with inky rivulets seeping out from his eyes, nose, and ears. His knees buckle and his body collapses, yet he remains suspended in the air, skewered by the creature's bladed tail.

The spectral beast, a grotesque vision of shadow and dread, reels in its paralyzed victim towards its cavernous, salivating maw. With a horrifying crunch, the creature drives its massive mandibles into the back of the man's head, the sound echoing as it begins its gruesome feast.

The Sterling Saga continues in *Tundra*… coming soon.

www.ingramcontent.com/pod-product-compliance
Lightning Source LLC
Chambersburg PA
CBHW020408110726
47899CB00006B/1903